The Toils of Language

The Toils of Language

Noah Jonathan Jacobs

IVAN R. DEE
CHICAGO

First published in 1990 by
NEW AMSTERDAM BOOKS
171 Madison Avenue
New York, NY 10016

First Printing

Published in 2009 by Ivan R. Dee, Publisher. The paperback
edition of this book carries
the following ISBN: 978-1-56663-789-3

Library of Congress Cataloging in Publication Data
Jacobs, Noah J. (Noel Jonathan), 1907–
The toils of language / Noah Jacobs.
p.   cm.
ISBN 0-941533-47-6
I. Language and languages.   I. Title.
P106.J27   1990
402—dc19   88-32952
CIP

This book is printed on acid-free paper.

Printed in the United States of America.

CONTENTS

Adam Naming the Beasts. From an English Bestiary,
Leningrad

I

Adam Naming the Animals in a Twelfth-Century Bestiary

IN THIS UNUSUAL BIBLICAL SCENE OUR FIRST ANCESTOR MAKES HIS APPEAR-
ance not as Rousseau's noble savage pruning the trees and watering the
flower beds of Eden or as Locke's indolent youth apricating in its
fragrant bushes, or as Hobbes' predatory *homo lupus,* the most destruc-
tive of all the animals, or as Dostoyevski's guilt-ridden underground
man, or as Karl Marx's dispossessed anonymous proletarian. The father
of the human race comes upon the scene as a prematurely aged scholar,
resembling the renowned Swiss alchemist, Theophrastus Bombastus
von Hohenheim, known as Paracelsus, or the great French zoologist,
Baron Cuvier, as he walked among the animals in the Jardin des Plantes.

He gives the impression of a man of destiny with high pretensions to originality, about to announce some basic principle of universal importance. He acts as if the world began with his arrival and existed for his sake. His advent had more than local significance. The unmistakable signs of his divine origin would have been recognized and acknowledged far beyond the cloistered walls of the Garden.

The cowering animals that marked time before Adam were too absorbed in the satisfaction of their appetites to challenge his supremacy and escort him across a bridge of words to freedom. Had they shown the slightest inclination for such an unstable metamorphosis, God would have lent them a helping Hand. They were too fearful of the Unknown to risk a rupture with their instincts and soon turned aside to sniff their way back to their secure lairs. No animal had the intellectual self-assurance to take possession of the world by means of symbolic forms unless it were, as the Scottish philosopher Lord Monboddo suggested, that patient architect, the beaver, or perhaps the semi-erect ape facing Adam and holding what appears to be an apple, a premonition of the pomological scandal that was to break out later in the day. Man was clearly singled out for the greatest benefits and destined to be master not only of Eden but of all nature: the sea divided before Moses, the sun stood still before Joshua, the ravens fed Elijah, the lions refused to devour Daniel, the whale spewed up Jonah, and the heavens opened up to Ezekiel:

> O what a world of profit and delight,
> Of power, of honour, and omnipotence,
> Is promis'd to the studious artisan!
> All things that move between the quiet poles
> Shall be at my command. Emperors and kings
> Are but obey'd in their several provinces,
> Nor can they raise the wind or rend the clouds.
> But his dominion that exceeds in this
> Stretcheth as far as doth the mind of man. . . .
> —Marlowe, *Dr. Faustus*, I.1

Who was this egregious biped that suddenly appeared among the animals—a zoological freak fallen from monkeyhood, a beast with brains? Where did he come from and what was his destination? He himself did not know, and he knew no one who did. Despite his high intellectual pretensions he knew remarkably little about himself beyond his name, his face (in the mirror) and the trivial contents of his pockets. His real self remained inarticulate and invisible. The hidden springs of his emotional life, the origin and value of his ideals, his need for justification and salvation, are impervious to intellectual illumination. The two most important events at the beginning and end of life, birth and death, are hidden in deepest darkness. Man can see the face of the watch, so to speak, perceive its moving hands and hear its ticking, but is unable to open the case. He can only surmise that such an ingenious contraption must have been put together by an intelligent Maker for a definite purpose, namely, to tell the time.

In pursuit of self-knowledge man lost himself in introspective mazes of self-deception, like one who steps out of his house, rings the doorbell and is surprised to find nobody home. The most intrepid explorers of the human heart—Solomon, Pascal, Dostoyevski, Freud—found it a dark jungle, impenetrable to the mind and the senses. "I do not know myself," Goethe said, "and may God keep me from such knowledge." Jesus knew who he was since God Himself, as Milton informs us, had told him: "My Father's voice/Audibly heard from heaven, pronounced me His." Yet he longed for public confirmation of his identity and anxiously kept asking his disciples: "Who do men say that I am. . . . who do you say that I am?" (Mark 8:27,29). The tormenting question of our identity keeps eluding us. "To be oneself," the Button Moulder told Peer Gynt, "is to kill oneself, and to write on the epitaph: Here lies no one."

On the extreme left side of the green we see Adam, still unaccustomed to his upright position, leaning against the trunk of a tree and holding in his right hand (not without a trace of vanity) a horny goose-quill poised in midair. Not a whip or cudgel to tame the beasts or a lyre to charm them, nor a brush and palette to depict them frolicking on the green, nor an abacus to take stock of his worldly goods, but a quill, as befits one who is about to engage in the rational activity of writing and see the world mirrored and transformed in a drop of ink! *Homo nascitur poeta,* man was born a poet. He took his stand outside Nature and pitted his solitary mind against her immutable laws, confident that his phantom creations in black ink would outlive the gilded monuments of princes:

> If this be error, and upon me prov'd.
> I never writ, nor no man ever lov'd.

Suspended from his left shoulder and extending beyond the confines of the margin we see the scroll on which Adam will soon write the names he gave the animals that passed before him and on whose endless blank surfaces posterity will set down its conflicting interpretations of the world, the record of its joys and torments, its triumphs and defeats and, if fortunate, "Lays of such delight,/That maids will sing them on their bridal night" (Byron). This was to be man's answer to the intolerable muteness of a silent universe that sustains him for a brief moment as consciousness and then absorbs him forever.

Man's mind is so constituted that it cannot remain content with mere observation, and it was not long before Adam felt an irresistible urge to transform the scroll's white surface. After a moment of uncertainty he began to decorate its borders, at first with graffiti and then, in a rough and ready fashion, with the names of the animals: the letter א *aleph,* representing the head of the ox; ג *gimel,* the foot of the camel, later followed by parts of the human body; כ *caf,* the palm of the hand; ק *kof,* the back of the head and spine; ש *shin,* a tooth—crude pictographic characters arranged on the scroll in alternate boustrophedonic lines, as a field is plowed by oxen. In all this, according to an early rabbinic account, Adam was aided by the letters formed by the phylacteries on the hand and back of the head, the knots and joints serving as mnemonic cues to recall the forms of the letters of the alphabet, a *memoria technica* similar to knots we tie in handkerchiefs to assist the memory. This curious view of the origin of writing is supported by the double meaning of "articulation," which refers to distinct joints and knots as well as to distinct sounds and syllables.

We have no exact knowledge of the nature of man's earliest writing. The scroll in Adam's hand is still untouched, and no trace of written marks can be detected even with the aid of a strong lens. The only information concerning the events of that fateful first morning in the Garden, besides the brief account in the second chapter of the book of Genesis, is derived from Dante's personal interview with the "Progenitor of our race" when the immortal Italian poet toured Paradise. Time had made considerable depredations in the Progenitor's appearance: his line of leverage had shifted from the middle to the big toe, a solitary tooth in the upper mandible gave him a droll look, and part of the apple that had stuck in his throat kept moving up and down as he spoke. He was nevertheless able to answer the questions put to him by the Interviewer, revealing that he last saw Eden 6,498 years ago, that he was evicted from the Garden less than seven hours after his arrival, and that the language he spoke was Hebrew. Few interviews in history have been so significant from the standpoint of time, place and subject matter. It is regrettable, however, that the poet in his haste failed to inquire into the nature of first man's written exercise. A plain description of the scribbling on the scroll, however fanciful or defective, would have afforded an invaluable insight into early man's mental development and a more powerful stimulus for linguistic studies than Wittgenstein's *Tractatus.*

One of the most striking features of the Naming Scene is the dramatic contrast between Adam clothed in his flowing robe and the naked animals before him. Animals are not conscious of being naked and have no need to conceal the intimacies of the body. It was for a long time assumed (on inconclusive evidence) that Adam's scholarly robe was originally designed to conceal the marks of his lost tail which, as an old midrash informs us, had been removed by God in order to fashion Eve, leaving man to this day with a useless coccyx.[1] Adam,

---

[1] A poetic version of this homiletical tale is provided by the Irish poet, Thomas Moore, in his *The Rabbinic Origin of Woman,* ca. 1820.

however, had no need to conceal the signs of decaudation. Caudal deprivation is not incompatible with man's dignity. The loss of a tail in man, like that of the foreskin in circumcision, is not a blemish but a mark of perfection.[2] A tail, when attached to an animal, is endowed with teleological significance, denoting in its possessor a knowledge of ends and the instinctive means to attain them. In the animal world an unadorned posterior is a misfortune, tantamount to a loss of face among humans. This *argumentum ex caude*, however, does not apply to man, who is free to choose his own ends and press forward to goals of his own making. The primary function of Adam's robe was not to conceal the absence of a tail but to cover his sex parts which had become provocatively exposed as a result of his perpendicularity.

Although covered by the robe and out of sight, man's sex parts were not out of mind. Now and then man would pause in his pursuit of power and culture, lift a small corner of the robe and then hastily re-cover the incriminating evidence of his animal origin. The hands of Esau that reached for a blessing, at once erotic and bewildering, were restrained by the voice of Jacob with its promise of culture and the artifices of civilized life. In these stolen glances of peeping guilt (scopophilia or Freudian *Schaulust*) Adam recognized something strange yet familiar, repressed and half-forgotten, an uncanny reminder of a place where he once tarried in his preconscious animal life. This perpetual covering and uncovering with the robe produced in man a congenital vacillation, a permanent rift between the body's speechless ecstasy and moral discipline, between a jungle of particularities and a desert of abstractions, between curiosity and inhibition, gratification and remorse—a complex cycle of revealment and concealment (Ger. *entbergen* has this double meaning) that involved him in a web of problems he could neither solve nor evade. He looked behind him to the green roots of his animal life (not without regret) and before him to the frail flower of culture (not without misgiving), to a world of history,

---

[2]To turn a defect into a virtue is called "alopecuria" (Gr. *alopekia* fox-mange, baldness) after the foxes in the fable who considered the loss of their tails to be a mark of beauty.

freedom and sin. This painful balancing effort at the center of two incompatible impulses taxed man's strength and sanity, giving him at times a pathetic, even comical, appearance.

In this irreconcilable duality we see the essential moral paradox of the human predicament. On the one hand, man is free to develop his mind in search of scientific truth and artistic creation, and on the other, he is punished for probing the mysteries of pure being, which is the realm of the gods. Man was expelled from Eden because he exercised his freedom to seek knowledge, and he was barred from returning to Eden because the acquisition of knowledge is interwoven with evil. Man's highest good offends the gods and must be paid for with suffering and guilt. "He who increases knowledge increases sorrow" (Eccles. 1:18): *know* rimes with *woe*.

This deep division in human nature is symbolized by the robe that Adam is wearing, his most striking characteristic that conceals and at the same time reveals the mysteries of the body. Clothes make the man. An ape dressed up as a king will be treated as a king. Majesty without the trappings of dress is a mere jest. An animal in trousers and a man without trousers are equally ridiculous and covered with derision. The endless improvisations of modes of dress—the judge's robe, the prisoner's garb, the monk's cowl, the soldier's uniform, the scholar's gown, Caesar's cloak, Lear's rags, and Shylock's gaberdine—betray (in the two senses of "deceive" and "exhibit") the character, profession and social position of the wearer. Man is wrapped up in make-believe and playacting as in a garment, often borrowed, ill-fitting and inappropriate to his station and person. Dress is not primarily designed to reveal the form of the body but to disguise it in accordance with tacit social conventions. To appear in borrowed dress not commensurate with one's social status is looked upon as burlesque or travesty (Fr. *travestir* change of dress as disguise) and is reserved for carnivals and mardi gras. Pickwick refused to appear at a fancy-dress ball in the character of Plato, Zeno, Epicurus or Pythagoras, who, like himself, were founders of clubs, humbly protesting that "as I cannot put myself in competition with these great men, I cannot presume to wear their dresses." Clothes can also be used as a social weapon, however, as they are by the dandy, the hippy or the nudist, for example, to challenge middle-class notions of utility, occupational dignity or fig-leaf propriety.

Can man throw off the robe, face the naked truth and regain his lost grace in the double sense of harmony of bodily movement and deliverance from sin? Is he under the spell of a blind life-force that keeps him from his real self, in bondage to interminable disguises and subterfuges, compelling him to take appearances for reality, words for things, *noblesse de robe* for *noblesse de coeur*?

The premature loss of his visible tail at one end and the acquisition of an invisible symbolic language at the other placed man at the center of two incompatible but equally imperious impulses, the vital power of blind instinct behind him and the luminous goals of unanticipated knowledge before him. Nature had not made adequate provision for this "beast with brains" who had outwitted her, and thus she remained indifferent, even hostile, to man's intellectual and moral aspirations. The imbalance between the human mind and inanimate nature is man's permanent predicament. It manifests itself throughout his biological evolution and in all aspects of his life. His unending task is to find the crucial line that divides the clod from the spirit, the wick from the flame and, if possible, a discernible principle of reconciliation. Are the two worlds related as clasp and hook, button and buttonhole (Leibniz's pre-established harmony), raw material and finished product (Kant), dancer and dance (Yeats), man and wife (in Blake's married land of Beulah), or imperceptibly blended as in a winepress (the highest wisdom of Browning's *Jochanan Hakkadosh*)? Moses without Sinai to support him would be feeble and apathetic; Sinai without Moses is bleak and meaningless.

II

The First Spelling Bee, or the Game of Life

AN ANCIENT RABBINIC HOMILY REPRESENTS THE NAMING OF THE ANIMALS as a verbal contest between Adam, the angels and the devil, presided over by the Lord himself as Divine Interlocutor. The angelic host, which numbered 301,655,722 according to the Cabbala, was soon disqualified and retired behind the Lord to watch the principals from the sidelines. Angels communicate in a diaphanous language bereft of all material density or sensible images and are hence too conceptual (i.e., conceited) to participate in spelling bees. Games of amusement are foreign to the angelic mood. Their principal function as God's executive arm is to carry out his decisions. The devil, who entered on horseback from the north, was the first to be called upon after lots had been drawn to determine the order of participation, but he failed to identify the first three animals that the Lord passed before the contestants, namely, the ox, the ass and the camel. Thereupon Adam, without hesitation, pronounced the correct names and was hailed the victor.

How did Adam contrive to win this verbal contest? He was no match for the devil. He had no models to emulate, no reference works or maps to consult, no inherited scheme of things to prepare him to enter the confused world of history. The devil, on the other hand, in his struggle with virtue had become a past master of ambiguity, prevarication, persiflage and scurrility. And yet he lost!

At this point we come upon the first of those strange coincidences of history which hint at the operation of a divine plan in all human movements, namely that the verbal duel in the Garden had been "fixed" by the presiding Interlocutor himself who revealed to Adam the correct answers by whispering in his ear the first letter of the name of the animal under consideration. This amazing particular is exegetically derived from the biblical verse "I will help you to speak, and I will tell you what to say" (Exod. 4:12), and iconographically corroborated in the *Adam and Eve Cycle,* Narthex Dome, San Marco, Venice, and also in Klagenfurt, Mus. Cod. VI, 19 (Millstatt Genesis), where God is shown presiding over the contest and secretly prompting Adam.

The devil was not prepared to be out-deviled by a divine ruse at the very beginning of his career, and it turned his initial enthusiasm into bitterness and ill will. Heckled by the unfriendly angelic host, he fled tantivy to the shades, taking the hindmost, vowing vengeance—not, however, before showing adam the ischial callosities on his backside as a gesture of contempt, at the same time emitting a crepitation of no small size that quickly filled the fragrant Garden. It is not recorded whether Adam had the presence of mind to answer in kind. For the only way to discomfit the devil, according to Luther, who dealt with this problem at first hand, was to fart directly into his nostrils and give him, as it were, a taste of his own medicine. This homeopathic remedy for exorcising the devil is illustrated in Goya's etching *Sopla* in which we see a noisome wind issuing from the naked posterior of a child that is being held by its feet and manipulated like a pair of bellows, ostensibly to light a fire in preparation for a bacchanalian feast. Adam did pursue the fleeing devil, however, with names like "Old Nick" and

"Auld Hornie," causing great laughter to be heard in the Garden for the first time.

It was not long before the devil returned to the Garden, this time to infect Eve with sin, the so-called theory of *inquinamentum,* which resulted in the expulsion of the primal pair from their native home and in the breakdown of the initial collaboration between God and man. We hear again of the devil at the time of the great Flood which he survived as a stowaway on Noah's Ark. During the voyage he bored a hole in the ship's bottom in an attempt to sink the human race, an infernal project that was defeated by the quick-witted hedgehog when it stuffed itself into the hole to prevent the water from rushing in. Modern man is faced with an equally grave peril that demands an immediate response, namely, the extinction of the human race. But no hedgehog will now save him, for he no longer believes in a merciful God who performs miracles for His creatures. God has been declared dead in our time, the victim of a fatal philosophical virus.

The devil's most successful undertaking was in connection with the Tower of Babel where he incited the builders to rebel by confusing their tongues. He also has other achievements to his credit: he invented paper money, dabbled in chemistry, wrote a large dictionary and learned to play all the musical instruments, with a marked preference for the French horn. As his work became more extensive he was obliged to employ a host of assistants, variously known as trolls, imps, hobgoblins, broggarts, kobolds, pixies and other demons in human shape, which he recruited at his main office in Kirkcaldy, Scotland, the birthplace of Adam Smith, for it is among the Scots that the devil enjoys the greatest popularity. One of the demons, known as Titivillus, who served as his moonshee, was assigned the task of collecting errors of speech, especially letters dropped by monks and nuns while reciting prayers. He put these letters in a bag that hung around his neck and delivered them every evening to his master at a special department known as the "Collection and Disposal of Verbiage," where the material was catalogued and the offending lapses duly registered.

Moral philosophers influenced by gnostic heresies reproach Adam for entering into collusion with God and participating in an unethical stratagem to defeat the devil. He should have allied himself with the devil and with those who defy the Omnipotent in the name of human freedom: Eve and the serpent, Cain, Sisyphus, Antigone and Prometheus. In the eyes of these moralists God is not our Father and we are not His children, either biologically or by adoption. He is a stern King whose laws are independent of man's welfare. When He expelled our First Ancestor from Eden, He left him not only penniless but in debt. He not only removed the oil from his lamp but He destroyed the wick and plunged man into a dark world of sin, stunned and half-crushed like a worm, while "He sits in heaven and laughs" (Ps. 2:4). A God who is deaf to the wail of human suffering, to the triumph of evil and the anguish of the innocent, is a wicked Deity. We owe this Deity no allegiance and we need not grovel before Him.

Are we then to love this God who is indifferent to our fate, who at Auschwitz "kept his right hand in his bosom" and refused to intervene with a saving miracle? Must we reconcile ourselves to a one-sided love, like that of a little girl for her doll? The moral world is ruled by the Parliament of Man without a sovereign: *vox populi vox dei*. We are brothers without a father, and we need no divine guidance to act morally. "Should we not continue in sin that grace may abound?" (Rom. 6:1)—*Pecca fortitur,* as Luther advised Melanchthon. God's commandments are worthy of obedience only if they conform to the rules of human reason, in which case He is superfluous. Did not God himself say of Israel, as reported in the Talmud (anticipating Kant): "Would that they had abandoned me, if only they would observe my Torah!"

Let us sabotage His creation, "the theater of His glory," abstain from marriage and procreation, and the illusory pleasures of a sinful world (the way of asceticism adopted by various heretical sects in the Middle Ages); or, being innocent and without guilt, let us indulge our appetites and the lusts of the flesh without fear of retribution (the way of libertinism followed by others), throw off the burden of the law and sin our way to moral freedom: "To the gallows with Moses!" This was the audacious slogan associated with the name of Johannes Agricola, the recording secretary at the disputation in 1519 between Martin Luther and Johann Eck, later the subject of a poem by Robert Browning:

And having thus created me,
  Thus rooted me, he bade me grow
Guiltless for ever, like a tree
  That buds and blooms, nor seeks to know
  The law by which it prospers so.
            —*Johannes Agricola in Meditation*

This ancient gnostic tradition that challenges God himself and His imperfect world, in which it perceives neither beauty nor order, has reappeared in the atheistic political ideologies of our century.

Adam was not inclined to follow this kakodoxical doctrine with its perversion of God the Father. He had no feelings of guilt; he had not resorted to theft and cunning in defiance of the gods as did Prometheus. His first impulse was to submit to the authority of the One who had placed him in a joyful Garden and guided his first steps. Faced with the decision of choosing between God and the devil, Adam acted in accordance with the first principle of practical politics, later vitiated by the growth of humanitarianism, namely, that in the struggle for survival, sentiments of generosity without powerful alliances can only lead to disaster. Under certain circumstances it may be prudent, even laudable, to deviate from prescribed rules. Bullfighters adhere to the rigorous prescriptions of their sport only because they are dealing with an "upright," incorruptible adversary and not with their fellow men, who in pursuit of selfish ends reveal a propensity for treachery, fraud and skulduggery. Present-day progressive minds reject this unflattering view of human nature (although there is sufficient evidence to support it) and recommend dialogue, unilateral concessions and empathy in dealing with an unprincipled enemy.

In those early days in the Garden it was more important for Adam to be on good terms with the Judge of the contest than to observe the rules of fair play. Now, fair play is an upper-class English concept derived from the playing fields of Eton, a concept congenial to an imperial power that is confident of ultimate victory—which is, however, seldom achieved without subterfuge and guile. The great men whose statues adorn our public squares did not acquire their power by being meek, fair, and truthful. As Neitzsche cynically remarked, "History treats almost exclusively of bad men who have later been declared good. Men in pursuit of power cannot afford to cultivate the recommended virtues"—"good guys finish last." Even saints sometimes find it necessary (convenient) to suspend moral laws so that, in conjunction with moods of deep contrition and self-abnegation, they often reveal a surprising absence of humility and human charity.

Although Adam was the oldest inhabitant of Eden, he was young in years, inexperienced and prone to errors of judgment. He had named the animals, his greatest single achievement, but his mind was too distracted by the novel excitements of the empirical world and rallied around no unifying core of fixed loyalties. Nevertheless, he could not postpone the proceedings in the Garden and wait until he would have more knowledge of the world. One always acts with insufficient knowledge or not at all, and in either case incurs guilt. A man who acts cannot reflect too long on the possible consequences of his action, for these are unpredictable and often contrary to his intentions. "The doer always acts without conscience; no one has a conscience except the spectator" (Goethe)—an observation repeated and followed by Bismarck. The consequences of an act are too complicated and cannot be formulated in advance: our footprints are always behind us. As the principal actor in this early drama, Adam could not remain neutral (indecisive), cry "No play!" and retire to the sidelines to watch the play as an amused spectator, a *Zaungast des Lebens*. The other actors, all ideally suited for the roles they were to play, had already made their appearance on the green stage. The props were in place, the traps set, and the curtain about to go up on the first of a succession of thrilling scenes in the great drama of life that was destined to have a long run until the end of time, a drama that some have found entertaining, others exasperating, and still others a tale told by an idiot, full of sound and fury, signifying nothing.

From God's intervention on behalf of man at the outset of his career we can derive a number of important pedagogical principles. The Lord could have named the animals himself and then have Adam learn the names by rote. This would have left man's mind unexercised and wholly dependent on ready-made formulas. The proper function of a teacher is to present problems and not solutions, to provide the yeast and not the whole loaf. On the other hand, to have Adam invent names for the animals by himself would be to abandon him to subjective whims and sudden impulses. Human language is too complicated a work for man to have originated alone without supplementary aid. The Lord therefore prompted Adam with the initial letter of the name of the animal that passed before him, thus providing him with an *a priori* principle not derived from his own meager experience and subjective speculations. The initial impulse came from God's revelation in the form of dark hints and cryptic allusions which remained to be broadened and refined by man's neverending interpretations: "The glory of God is to keep things hidden but the glory of kings is to fathom them" (Prov. 25:2). Having provided the first letter, however, God did not abandon man and leave him alone to bear "the heavy and weary weight of all this unintelligible world" (Wordsworth), but patiently awaited man's creative response which, however feeble, incongruous or rebellious, was destined to illumine and transfigure the world of His creation.

The primary purpose of the contest in the Garden was not to defeat the enemy. An elaborate game with the pretence of fair play was not needed to achieve this predetermined outcome. The real purpose of making life a kind of game was to keep the weapons of the contestants bright for the struggle of survival, to defeat boredom and dispel the solemnity that broods over Nature, to mark man's triumph over her arbitrary and disorderly ways and to compensate him for the abasement he suffers at her hands. Above all, play establishes links of unity and modes of cooperation between the human and divine, a middle ground where the two interpenetrate and nourish one another in the common work of salvation. The element of play is an indispensable ingredient in all aspects of civilized life: in warfare, courtship, bullfighting, politics and religion (we are still conscious of the close relation between *holiday* and *holy day*). The notion of life as a game was already recognized by Plato (*Laws,* vii.796):

What then is the right way of living? Life must be lived as a play, playing certain games, making sacrifices, singing and dancing, and then man will be able to propitiate the gods and defend himself against his enemies, and win the contest.

The most disconcerting aspect of the Garden contest is God's need to employ deception to save man from being defeated by the devil. The problem becomes more perplexing with God's continued deceptions after the Fall, when He had withdrawn his Presence and man was on his own. In his great philosophical work, *The Guide of the Perplexed* (1190), Maimonides justifies "God's deceit" as always undertaken for man's own good. Thus, when God "stole" a rib from Adam in order to fashion Eve, the word "stole" is to be understood in the sense of a thief who comes in the night, steals a silver jug and leaves a gold one in its stead. The Christian doctrine of Incarnation, according to Gregory the Great, is likewise based on a deceptive stratagem employed by God, who, repenting of his severe punishment in banishing Adam from Paradise, commanded His Son to disguise his divine nature and appear on earth in human form and redeem sinful mankind with his expiatory sacrifice—a beneficent deception whereby the Old Adam was replaced by the risen Christ, reprobate Eve by the Virgin Mary, the Garden of Eden by Gethsemene, and the cursed tree by the wood of the cross. God wants the truth, but not as we mortals know it. His truth operates by means of concealment, subterfuge and deception. It is not man but *Dieu trompeur* who writes the scenarios, of which he has an infinite variety.

The secular version of this theological explanation of "God's deceit" is Hegel's well-known principle of "the cunning of reason" whereby men's passions are used for ends incomprehensible to the finite human intellect which imagines it is following its own pleasurable ends while in truth serving the concealed purposes of a higher order. Hegel's principle is better known to English readers as "private vices, public benefits," the theme of Bernard Mandeville's *The Fable of the Bees* (1714), originally called *Knaves Turn'd Honest,* described in its day as "the wickedest cleverest book in the English language." The mechanism that turns private vices into public benefits was named by Adam

Smith in the early days of capitalism as "the invisible hand" which secretly promotes the common good by relying on the spirit of competition among men and their love of wealth, openly acknowledged and pursued with an eye to prudent investments. A now forgotten theologian, Abraham Tucker, a contemporary of Adam Smith who wrote under the pseudonym of Edward Search, confidently identified this "invisible Hand" as belonging to God who is to be conceived, according to this quaint theory, as the managing Director of a "universal cosmic bank," as it were, in which all our good deeds are deposited and whose general stock we, the shareholders, have a natural interest to guard and augment.

The crude dogmatic form in which these theories are generally expressed emphasizes the benefits of personal ambition and unfettered self-development without deploring their pernicious effects or seeking their amelioration. They overlook man's altruistic impulses, his attachment to social order, his docile submission to political systems and legal restraints, often at the cost of immediate pleasures. In their milder forms, however, these theories have been found less objectionable, especially in the sphere of politics, where self-interest and cupidity are taken for granted as impulses deeply rooted in all individuals, indeed as the only human traits that can be relied upon with certainty to form a moral consensus and a common basis for governing people. It is assumed that we can live and prosper best if we confine our opinions and sympathies to the private sphere and let ourselves be guided in the public domain by a spirit of enlightened self-interest while trusting in the hidden purposes of a benign Providence, a higher Reason or invisible Hand.

The doctrine that man acts only out of self-interest has been defended by a long line of moral philosophers. Self-interest is the yeast in the human dough, "the barbed hook baited with the illusion of progress" (Conrad). When we intend to do good "we feign a new act of the mind" (Hume); that is, we assume a sanctimonious pose and invent altruistic motives for our actions. This view of human nature has been severely criticized as disguised hedonism that "tears man out of heaven and puts him in a sty" (Berkeley) and creates a society whose ideal is the ruthless man of affairs: Balzac's *héros métallique*, Bounderby in Dickens's *Hard Times,* or our own prudential Benjamin Franklin, "the Philistine whose God was a heavenly storekeeper" (Baudelaire).

One of the severest critics of the utilitarian doctrine was Dostoyevski, who represents an extreme conservative view of man's nature. We erroneously assume that men are made happier by shorter working hours, early retirement and more leisure, which only bring greater responsibilities from which men flee. Human suffering cannot be eliminated by social reforms or violent revolution, for no political order can have the necessary knowledge to master the complexities of the human predicament. Marx's famous dictum, inscribed on his gravestone, that philosophers have hitherto tried to understand the world but must now try to change it, seems both blasphemous and futile. In Spenser's *The Faerie Queen* (Bk. V) we find an interesting description of a giant who, with a huge pair of scales in his hands, boasts that he can straighten out God's disorderly world, equalize mountains and valleys, remove injustices—and who fails disastrously. It is therefore best to leave the world to the inscrutable workings of an invisible Power that reconciles the discordant elements in society without our knowledge. It is presumptuous of the adherents of the various historical movements to profess to know its providential designs as to who is to inherit the earth—the meek of the New Testament (Toynbee), the heroic German nation (Hegel), the down trodden proletariat (Marx) or the physically fittest (Darwin):

> . . . when will their presumption learn
> That in the unreasoning progress of the world
> A wiser spirit is at work for us,
> A better eye than theirs, most prodigal
> Of blessings, and most studious of our good,
> Even in what seem our most unfruitful hours?
> —Wordsworth, *The Prelude,* V

The harsh judgment of the poet is directed against his Victorian contemporaries who had lost their faith in Providence and looked to historical experience as a guide to social redemption. To the poet, truth does not reveal itself in the confusing and untrustworthy lessons of history, but in a mood of "wise passiveness," when the meddling intellect relaxes its assault on the world and we enter the twilight zone of "still life" (Schopenhauer's favorite oxymoron) in a half-slumbering numbness conducive to poetical composition. To regard the promptings of the human heart and its fleeting moods as the ultimate source of the moral act, however, is to mistake the thermometer which measures fever for the fever itself or to confuse scratching with the itch. If we cannot trust the binding norms of moral conduct provided by religious faith or by historical experience, can we trust the wayward sentiments of the human heart, that foul cavern which is "deceitful above all things and exceeding weak" (Jer. 17:9)?

Adam on a twelfth-century Byzantine ivory panel, seated before a stylized palm tree, apparently before the creation of Eve. His dejected appearance illustrates God's words: "It is not good that man should be alone" (Genesis 2.18).

III

Woman as Inspiration or Hindrance

THIS DOUBLE VIEW OF WOMAN IS REFLECTED IN TWO REPRESENTATIONS, both of the twelfth century, in the Naming Scene of the first chapter and in the Byzantine panel before us. In the former we see a self-sufficient Adam alone in the Garden without Eve and hence, according to the so-called heremetic doctrine that forms the basis of the monastic orders, doubly blessed in two paradises—"Two Paradises 'twere in one/To live in Paradise alone" (Andrew Marvell, "The Garden"). Man here appears capable of determining his own destiny without a help-mate, content to live among the fountains and grottoes of Eden, skipping along its leafy walks and humming bits of barnyard melodies. There is nothing in this bucolic scene to suggest that Adam was dissatisfied with his single state. The Himalayan air of the Garden with its healing silence and pleasant smells disposed his mind to solitary pleasures. He was content with his frugal diet of milk, nuts, a bit of avocado and an occasional egg, eaten alone alfresco, undisturbed by the clamorous demands and intrusions of domestic life.

In the Byzantine panel, on the other hand, we see a disconsolate Adam overcome by a spirit of melancholy unknown to the animals who live joyously unless frightened by man. Hunched on a rocky stool (privy?), his heavy head leaning on his right arm and his toes gripping the earth, he bears a striking resemblance to Rodin's *The Thinker,* also known as "the metaphysician of the privy seat." The long periods of brooding over his solitary state were punctuated by vacant yawns and visions of a tender wife with "soft dimpled hands, white neck, and creamy breast" (Keats), someone to astonish and charm him and to share his ample possessions.

Adam is here faced with a profound paradox of the human condition, the dialectic of solitude. He could not live content alone or with another. He had a simultaneous desire for union and singularity, for attachment and withdrawal. Part of his being longed for female companionship, domestic bliss, and progeny to continue his name, while another part feared the narrow interests and entanglements of family life. Philo of Alexandria, who believed that man though fallen was not wholly irrational, informs us that Adam had objected to the creation of Eve when he first heard of it; and it was only after he had eaten the aphrodisiac apple that he was seized with an immoderate desire for sexual intercourse as a remedy for concupiscence. Man had to be deceived by a higher Reason whose hidden aim was the propagation of the species, which takes precedence over the rational considerations of the individual or, as a rabbinic dictum puts it: "If it were not for the evil impulse man would never marry, beget, build a house or engage in trade." The Lord therefore caused a deep sleep to fall upon Adam—"when the soft hand of sleep had closed the latch/On the tired household of corporal sense" (Wordsworth)—and removed a rib from his sinister side, the crookedest, "which rarely He refined/And thereof made the mother of mankind." She appears to have been made too hastily and, according to Freud, incomplete in a significant detail. Mencken, who had studied the subject at first hand, expresses the extreme negative view regarding her esthetic construction, namely, that "in comparison with woman the average milkjug or even cuspidor is an object of gratifying design." Nevertheless, in Adam's eyes she was the tender wife he had dreamed of. With all her blemishes, God made woman the object of man's rapture and implanted in the female bosom the means of his redemption. It was evidently His clear design that human beings should reach full spiritual development in pairs.

No matter what Eve looked like, Adam saw in her a Helen, fairer than the evening star, and he was eager to win her favors with humble services and appease her insatiable appetite for frippery and brummagem. Little did he realize in his ecstatic state that this coy maiden would soon enter his house, rearrange its contents, demand a full share of all his possessions and life's earnings, insist on constant conjugal passion and lifelong fidelity. A new disturbing element had entered his life involving a radical shift from egotism to tuism, from quiet contemplation to tumultuous passion, from tender monologues of subjective certainty to domestic altercations with endless contradictions and recriminations. The presence of a third party, a matchmaker, a Peeping Tom as a *tertius gaudens* who could reap the benefit of their discord, would have relieved the intolerable strain of prolonged intimacy. As it was, Nature, in pursuit of her own ends (the propagation of the species), removed the sex organs from his conscious control so that conjugation became a matter of frenzied urgency. How else could Adam have been persuaded to enter into such a hazardous relationship?

It has therefore been part of ancient wisdom to protect this slippery arrangement between the sexes with strong prescriptions designed to confine its pudendal activity to the marriage-bed, and then only as a *remedium concupiscentia*. Many sensitive men have conceived a distaste for the sexual act furtively performed *inter faeces et urinas,* as it is described (usually with disgust) by theologians and poets from St. Augustine to Dean Swift and Yeats. Fastidious husbands in Victorian England wore a sort of heavy undershirt in bed, known as a *chemise cagoule,* provided with a suitably placed opening through which they could impregnate their wives without lascivious heat and with a minimum of guilt and pleasure. Even the great ethical philosopher of the Enlightenment, Immanuel Kant, subordinated the amative to the propagative principle in marriage, which he defined, to the chagrin of his idealistic admirers, as "the mutual lease of the sexual organs," whereby the two partners connive to do one another a good turn or, as the French idiom has it, *"nous nous faisons une politesse."*

Marriage is thus an economic and social institution and only peripherally connected with sex, and hence not the best avenue for intellectual or moral self-expression. Many prudent men have chosen solitude rather than "With one chained friend, perhaps a jealous foe,/The dreariest and longest journey go" (Shelley). In one of his *Letters,* John Keats wrote: "I hope I shall never marry. Though the most beautiful creature were waiting for me at the end of a journey or a walk . . . my happiness would not be so fine as my solitude is sublime . . . the roaring of the wind is my wife and the stars through the window-pane are my children." Even the most practical of men, Robinson Crusoe, was able to lead a fruitful and industrious life on his desert island without the benefit of a woman, and chose a man he called Friday to be his ideal companion. In his interpretation of the Biblical phrase "a help meet unto Adam," St. Augustine points out that the creation of another *man* would have been more suitable both as a tiller of the soil and as a companion, for which he is chided by Milton for "rusticity in the affairs of the heart." Milton himself, however, expresses the same thought with even greater virulence in the *cri de coeur* he put in Adam's mouth:

> Oh why did God,
> Creator wise that peopled highest Heaven
> With spirits masculine create at last
> This novelty on earth, this fair defect
> Of nature and not fill the world at once
> With men as angels without feminine
> Or find some other way to generate
> Mankind . . . .
> —*Paradise Lost,* X

Uninspired biblical critics, eager to detect imperfections in man's early history, however farfetched, have been unduly disturbed by the absence of fish in the Garden lineup when the animals were being named. In his grand epic Milton answered these carping critics by pointing out that Eden was inland and that the "dreary-mouthed, gaping wretches of the sea could not be summoned from their watery residence to draw the thinner air." Although elegantly expressed, this argument holds no water. Fish have been known to undertake short nuptial pilgrimages overland and even to climb trees. Adam did not name the fish because he was not commissioned to do so, probably because of the difficulty of pronouncing ichthyic names. Many animals were not named for the same reason: the dziggetai, the hippopotamus and the wurmb among others. Some animals were not yet in existence. The pig and the cat, for example, were only created during the Deluge on Noah's Ark, as a plausible rabbinic homily informs us, where the pig was formed from the elephant's trunk to dispose of the accumulated garbage, and the cat sneezed forth by the lion to rid the boat of rats.

The absence of Eve from the Naming Scene is a more serious omission. Although not visible she *was* present, combing her hair under a tree beyond the ha-ha at the rear of the animal procession, waiting to be selected by Adam as his bride. For the primary purpose of the animal parade was not to provide names for the marchers but to serve as a kind of *Brautschau,* or bridal procession, in which prospective brides submitted themselves to Adam's inspection. This bold rabbinic interpretation is derived from the circumstance that the same verse in which Adam names the animals concludes with the words: "but for Adam there was not found a help meet [helpmate] unto him." Adam indicated his rejection of the four-footed bridal candidates that passed before him by pronouncing their names with a tone of disgust and impatience accompanied by a wave of the hand as if chasing away a bad odor. The unsuccessful candidates thus received their names in the very act of being spurned. This obscure homily of the origin of human speech anticipated the modern neural theory, the so-called interjectional or pooh-pooh theory, according to which language is basically not an objective description of the external world but an affective activity for unburdening the emotions. In naming the animals Adam gave vent to the disturbing affections which the dumb beasts evoked in him. He did not give them names; he called them names.

It is disconcerting to contemplate the striking modifications in our nature had first man's ardor, misguided by some momentary fever, preferred a scandalous mésalliance with one of the horizontal marchers in the procession. The human imagination has pictured such a commingling of the animal and the human in satyrs, harpies, centaurs, sphinxes and werewolves. Had God meant man for such a disparaging union he would have left him to roam the forest on all fours. Better a vow of celibacy that would make him a eunuch for the kingdom of Heaven than stoop to the indignity of such a left-handed union! Fortunately, Adam spied Eve at the end of the procession, and he greeted her not with the rude interjections that accompanied the names of the animals—ugh, pshaw, phew, pfui—but with an ecstatic tristich spoken *con amore:* "This time it is bone of my bone and flesh of my flesh." And Eve answered his greeting not with a purr or growl but with tender notes of joy and hope. The animals in the parade were a spectacle to be viewed and reviewed, and then branded with sharp-edged nouns that revealed their common traits; Eve was a vision to be recognized and admired with ever-changing adjectives. Human speech now entered into its spectacular social role, involving the art of listening and the risk of contradiction.

The theme of woman as inspiration or hindrance reappears in connection with Eve's participation in the creation of language, a subject on which men of learning, not all of them unbiased, have advanced confident opinions. Dante found it unseemly that so exalted an act as human speech should first have proceeded from a woman and assures us that Eve was silent throughout the Naming Scene, which is highly improbable. This manly opinion is not shared by Mark Twain, who had little respect for the father of mankind whom he pictured as a good-natured nincompoop, unable to tell a P-cock from a Q-cumber, an ant from a pheasant, or a puss from an octopus, mistaking the walrus for a horse, the owl for a feathered cat, and the zebra for a striped ass. Of grammatical gender he had not the vaguest notion, especially where a rapid or obscure mode of propagation escaped detection, as in the erotic entanglements of snapping turtles, salacious elephants or retro-mingent camels. Eve looked upon his linguistic ineptitude with half-concealed amusement, but she never left his side and prompted him at every turn.

Adam's linguistic obtuseness was especially evident when it came to naming the flowers. At this stage his practical mind had little experience with beauty. A primrose by the river's brim was just a yellow primrose to him. Flowers merely served as a colorful backdrop for the Animal Parade. Did he envy their independence of animal life, their quiet absorption of dew and air, their silent sexless reproduction? Did he detect in their ephemeral existence a foreboding of the fate soon to overtake him? It was Eve who appreciated these gaudy jewels that grew at her feet and filled the air with fragrance and who gave them their names—the darling daisy, the coquettish pansy, the narcotic daffodil, the impatient touch-me-not, the kiss-me-at-the-garden-gate and Adam's needle (now the state flower of New Mexico)—and they in turn saluted her as a sister flower, begging to be crushed under her foot that they might exude their rich odors:

> *Eve, fleur de ma vie, o ma femme, o*
> *Salut, fleur de beauté, ma soeur!*
> *Et que si ton pied nous écrase*
> *Nous ressentons comme une extase*
> *De volupté.*

In the utopian societies envisaged by male writers, such as Bacon's *New Atlantis,* Hermann Hesse's *The Glass Bead Game,* or Vaclav Havel's *New Memorandum,* women are excluded from the linguistic process in the life of the community since it is one of the principal aims of these societies to cleanse language of its allegedly feminine elements—its idle chatter, perverse logic, nagging repetitions and shrill insistence—and thus make it more amenable to the contours of the astringent masculine mind. The ideal society was to be governed by a perfect language of abstract signs, bereft of all sensible ingredients. The mother tongue was treated as primitive tribes were commanded to treat their captive women: cut their hair, pare their nails, and divest them of all ornaments and accidental extravagances. In this cleansing activity, which demands discrimination, detachment and quiet analysis, women are superfluous and even a hindrance.

The linguistic reforms adopted by these utopian societies soon came to naught. They only succeeded in distracting men from their plain civic duties and domestic responsibilities, and in the end undermined human speech as an instrument of social communication. To speak a language cleansed of all impurities, errors and passions is like living in a house with immaculate radiators and accurate thermometers but with no furnace. On the other hand, similar attempts made by women to exclude men from *their* society were always successful, as we find, for example, in the three plays of Aristophanes: *Thesmophoriazusae, Lysistrata* and *Ecclesiazusae*. The women in these plays are primarily interested in achieving two practical goals, the termination of the war and the introduction of communal sexual intercourse. Having decided on a fixed strategy to attain these ends, they entered upon the execution of their plans with an enviable intuitive knowledge of the forces that govern human conduct and with a singleness of purpose unhampered by feelings of pity or fair play. The astonishing vigor displayed by women in the pursuit of their ends is illustrated in DeMaupassant's famous story, "Bed Number Twenty-nine," in which the mistress of a wounded army officer confesses as she lies dying of syphilis that after being captured she had infected as many of the enemy as possible, uttering with her last breath the patriotic boast: "I killed more of the enemy than you!" A number of such instances of patriotic zeal by prostitutes who infected the enemy to save their country have been recorded and discussed from various points of view. Enlightened theologians are of the opinion that this form of bacterial warfare, as it were, is not to be counted as a sin of fornication or lechery since it is undertaken for the love of the fatherland, and is therefore not condemned by the Church, provided that the prostitutes derive no pleasure from their heroic task.

Are women less sensitive to language than men? They seem to be generally more aware of violations of rules of grammar and orthography, less given to rude expressions, to mumbling, stuttering, hemming and hawing, quicker to detect verbal pretence and, when not in the grip of a strong emotion, display a readier wit and deeper knowledge of human nature. Have there been women renowned for puns, aphorisms, (bawdy) limericks or other forms of malicious wit that afford momentary pleasure and inflict lasting wounds? (Cattiness reflects a lack of sympathy and is not a literary genre.)[1] Is a woman constitutionally equipped to become a master player in the aggressive game of chess, a game that re-enacts the Oedipus drama in which victory is achieved by murdering the king? Do we know any women who enjoy clowning, horseplay or practical jokes (e.g., a hotfoot), or who slap their sides in paroxysms of mirth laughing at their own jokes? Women sometimes engage in a piece of roguery or tomfoolery, although seldom against members of their own sex, whom they fear more than men, but then it lacks the broad grin and lighthearted aggressiveness of the male. Can we conceive of a female Falstaff, a Charlie Chaplin or a Don Quixote tilting at windmills? Are there in the annals of world literature female counterparts of Melville's Bartleby, Valéry's M. Teste or Goncharev's Oblomov, characters who led a purely verbal existence, absorbed in their own thought processes and in the sound of lifeless words? Did a woman ever suffer from *Sprachschreck,* the loss of confidence in the power of verbal expression, and cast aside the net of words to "walk barefoot into reality" (Wallace Stevens)?

Women are said to have more tongue than men. But what woman could vie with the talking powers of Carlyle, Diderot, Strindberg and Karl Kraus or with such literary characters as Sam Weller, Uncle Toby and the Ancient Mariner, all garrulous men who brooked neither interruption nor contradiction in an untiring effort to vex and annoy their listeners? Nevertheless, a woman needs the reassuring sound of the

---

[1]No figure except her own, as one wit put it, is used more often by women for purposes of dissimulation than that of *accismus* (pronounced *aksismus*), the figure of speech whereby one coyly refuses what one earnestly desires, e.g., Caesar's refusal of the crown three times. Fame is sought by seeming to spurn it—"To earn it by disdaining it/ Is Fame's consummate fee" (Emily Dickinson).

spoken word. Speech, however imperfect, is preferable to silence, and she is determined to speak, whether listened to or not:

> And speak I will. I am no child, no babe,
> Your betters have endur'd me say my mind,
> And if you cannot, best you stop your ears.
> —Katherine in *The Taming of the Shrew,* IV.3

Feminine volubility is checked only during courtship, a period of deep distrust in language. All talk, especially of an intellectual nature, is a blight to romance and fatal to sexual intimacy. The talk that inspires lovers is playful and noncognitive, suggestive of sexual intentions, designed to create an atmosphere of irresponsibility. Women sometimes *pretend* to fall in love with brilliant talkers, but they generally require more tangible proof of man's devotion, bold acts in which he risks life and limb in their behalf. In *Richard III,* Anne at first spurns the audacious marriage proposal of the royal rogue, made over the hearse of her husband, whom he has just murdered and she yields only when he threatens to take his life in despair, gives her his sword and bares his neck to her hatred. In some primitive societies suitors are required to undergo ordeals, such as sitting on thorns, putting out blazes by urination, wrestling with one's prospective mother-in-law or submitting to the dreaded ordeal of *vagina dentata,* which sometimes conceals poisonous snakes that prove fatal to the unsuspecting lover. Sustained rational discourse is disconcerting and fatiguing to lovers who prefer to demonstrate their delight in *le baratin d'amour,* in stolen glances or *oeillades,* "the petty larceny of the optics" (Meredith), in playful silence punctuated by apprehensive sighs and whispers:

> We like sepulchral statues lay;
> All day, the same our postures were,
> And we said nothing all the day.
> —John Donne, *Extasie*

People who sincerely desire to understand one another need only few words. The two lovers in Tolstoy's *Anna Karenina* (IV.3) are able to communicate without words, anticipating their thoughts by enigmatic hints conveyed by random letters of the alphabet. In an oft-quoted passage in his *Diary of a Writer*, Dostoyevski describes a conversation carried on by six drunkards that consisted of only one (obscene) word uttered with varying inflections and reinforced with appropriate gestures, whereby they were able to express all their thoughts and the entire gamut of their emotions: anger, joy, contempt, surprise and disappointment.

Incriminating evidence of male malefaction has been sought for and found in the vocabulary of our language: words at first applied to men and then unfairly to women (shrew, harlot, milliner); diminutive feminine names derived from the masculine suggesting an inferior status (Henrietta/Henry, Pauline/Paul, Juanita/Juan), the prototype of which is the formula pronounced by the bride at a Roman wedding: *Ubi tu Gaius, ego Gaia.* Feminine forms have been generally derived from the masculine—duke/duchess, goat/nanny goat, Span. *muchacho/muchacha,* Ger. *Hund/Hündin*—instead of independent suppletion forms: uncle/aunt, boy/girl, dog/bitch; exceptions to masculine precedence are: cat/tomcat, goose/gander, widow/widower. Some feminine names have been degraded to common nouns: Juliet/jilt, Dorothy/doll, Gunhild/gun, Joan/jug, Margaret/magpie. Man's domineering impulse has been detected even in his pet names for women: honey, sugar, sweetie pie—regarded as a patronizing deference of uxorious husbands who refer to their wives as "my better half" or "helpmate" and to women in general as "the fair sex" (referring to complexion and not to the sense of fair play). German pet names for women are derived more realistically from wild life: *Mäuschen* mousie, *Kätzchen* kitty, *Täubchen* dovey. Luther's affectionate term for his little daughter was *"kleine Hure"* since in the sixteenth century "whore" had not yet lost its root meaning (Lat. *carus* dear) and its etymological relation to "charity" and "caress."

Attempts to erase the linguistic traces of male injustices that have crept into our language are misconceived. The "man" in *spokesman, manhole, penmanship, snowman* (in Russian snow woman, *babushka*) is no more an indication of male malevolence than the "man" in the moon. There is no point in seeking feminine forms for *surgeon, orator, tyrant, charlatan,* or even in inventing forms for *boisterous, heehaw, patronize (girlsterous, shehaw, matronize).* A sensible woman is not concerned with the masculine root of "dominion" (Lat. *dominus* master, lord) as long as she can exercise it, nor with the origin of "pants" (from St. Pantaleone, a stock character in Italian comedy who wore long trousers) as long as she can wear them. The efforts of ethnic or private groups to delete words that they find offensive can only impoverish our vocabulary without reducing mutual recrimination or advancing the cause of tolerance. The Dutch would object to *Dutch courage* (induced by drinking) or *Dutch host* (one who is drunk by the time the guests arrive), the Welsh to *welshing* (cheating), the Chinese to *yellow streak,* the Bulgarians to *bugger,* the SPCA to *asinine, catty, silly goose,* etc. It is wiser to accept the derogatory word and redeem it by one's conduct, as have the Quakers, a name first applied in derision to those who shake and quake while praying, or the Methodists, a name that ridiculed their methodical habits, or the Old Contemptibles, the small British Expeditionary Force in France during the First World War, which took its name from the Kaiser's sneer at England's "contemptible little army."

Linguistic deficiency is not identical with moral turpitude. Obtuseness in language is not a character defect. That a man's morals improve in direct relation to his linguistic proficiency is far from self-evident. The fault is not with language: "A crab by any other name would not forget its way to the sea" (Zen proverb). Injustices are to be found in life and not in dictionaries:

> . . . but will any man say that, if the words whoring, drinking, cheating, lying, stealing, were, by an act of parliament, ejected out of the English tongue and dictionaries, we should awake the next morning chaste and temperate, honest and just, and lovers of truth? Is this a fair consequence? Or, if the physicians would forbid us to pronounce the words pox, gout, rheumatism and stone, would that expedient serve, like so many talismans, to destroy the diseases themselves?"
>
> —Swift, *The Abolishing of Christianity*

Evidence of male tyranny derived from linguistic sources is not a reliable guide in assessing the relative degrees of wickedness in the battle of the sexes. In the eternal seesaw of domination and submission that characterizes the insecure relationship between men and women it is reasonable to assume that both have suffered equally at each other's hands, although an impartial observer of the contemporary scene would be inclined to believe (privately) that the conjugal torment suffered by men is more malignant. The crown of martyrdom is not the exclusive glory of women. Is there no such thing as female tyranny? Are there not heavy responsibilities connected with male privileges? The present author cannot venture an authoritative opinion, however modest, concerning the merits of this quarrel, for it has been his fortune, both good and bad, to live alone without the solace of constant female companionship. Nothing is more conducive to peace of mind than to have no opinion on this subject. Judgment in this matter must be left to the highest competent powers, such as those, for example, who appear in Hohan Lauw's painting, "The Parliament in Heaven" (1681), in which we see the culprits of Eden, Adam and Eve, being tried before God, the Holy Ghost and Christ, the *advocati diaboli* being Truth and Justice, and the attorneys for the defense, Peace and Mercy. On the table before them are the pieces that have been placed in evidence: the fatal apple and the Law of Moses. The verdict will be rendered on the day when Mercy and Truth will meet together (Ps. 85), a verdict we await with confidence and equanimity.

Woman's attitude to language may be described as fiduciary, or the word as promise. The binding character of language is evident in the root meaning of words relating to marriage: to betroth or plight one's troth (AS *plight,* Ger. *pflicht* obligation; AS *treowth* truth) is a promise to *wed* (AS *weddian* to pledge; Ger. *wetten* to wager) and to undertake the duties of a spouse (Lat. *spondere* to promise). Etymological corroboration, although reassuring, needs to be implemented by more reliable means if women are to hold men to their promises: *vivat verbum, pereat homo.* A word is not to be taken lightly: "Why, sir, her name's a word, and to dally with that word might make my sister wanton" (*Twelfth Night,* III.1). The words "I do" in the marriage ceremony are not just words but an act, a performance, a pledge to enact a promised role. This makes all the difference between mating and marriage, a difference eloquently expressed by Mrs. Antrobus to her husband in Thornton Wilder's play, *The Skin of Our Teeth* (Act II):

> I didn't marry you because you were perfect. I didn't even marry you because I loved you. I married you because you gave me a promise. . . . (She takes off her ring and looks at it). That promise made up for your faults. And the promise I gave you made up for mine. Two imperfect people got married and it was the promise that made the marriage. . . . And when our children were growing up, it wasn't a house that protected them; and it wasn't our love that protected them—it was that promise.

In his Bryn Mawr lecture, "The Question of Our Speech" (1905), Henry James appealed to his female listeners as the custodians of culture (the men being too busy making money) not to indulge in thoughtless speech, reminding them that fidelity to the word is indispensable to the institution of marriage. Truth is anchored in our trust in man and not in his linguistic instruments. His credibility precedes the logical correctness of his assertions. The question is: Are his intentions honorable? Can he be relied upon to fulfill his obligations? Do his words conform to his social position and public character? A knowledge of words is in itself no guarantee of a corresponding intellectual comprehension, much less of a desire to live by them. Trust precedes knowledge. An apt illustration of this important truth is provided by one of Kierkegaard's parables:

> A traveling circus once broke into flames just after it had encamped outside a Danish village. The manager turned to the performers who were already dressed for their acts and sent the clown to call the villagers to help put out the fire, which could not only destroy the circus but might race through the dry fields and envelop the town itself. Dashing pell-mell to the village square, the painted clown shouted to everyone to come to the circus and help put out the fire. The villagers laughed and applauded this novel way of tricking them into coming to the big top. The clown wept and pleaded. He insisted that he was not putting on an act but that the town really was in mortal danger. The more he implored the more the villagers howled

... until the fire leaped across the fields and spread to the town itself. Before the villagers knew it, their homes had been destroyed.

(Quoted in Harvey Cox's *The Secular City,* New York, 1966, p. 247)

We now pause to pay tribute to two ancient women, one Greek and one Hebrew, whose reputations deserve to be rescued from the opprobrium heaped upon them by generations of chroniclers, poets and preachers. The name of Xantippe, Socrates' wife, has been made synonymous with an ill-tempered shrew (Ger. *Zank* quarrel, altercation) and has received little sympathy from readers of Greek history. Socrates is said to have courted death at his trial by making an ineffectual defense in order to escape from her. We tend to forget, however, that he spent most of the time philosophizing in the marketplace barefoot, that he neglected his domestic duties, sang ribald songs and ran after flute wenches. His unpleasing appearance is described by Rabelais in the prologue to his famous work, relying on the testimony of Alcibiades:

> ... judging by his exterior, you would not have given an onion skin for him. He was ill-shaped, ridiculous in carriage, with a nose like a knife, the gaze of a bull and the face of a fool. His ways stamped him as a simpleton, his clothes as a bumpkin. Poor in fortune, unlucky when it came to women, hopelessly unfit for all office in the Republic, forever laughing, forever drinking neck to neck with his friends, forever hiding his divine knowledge under a mask of mockery. . . .

This inspired pot-bellied freak, however, was reputed to have had a second wife named Myrto of whom Xantippe was inordinately jealous. Myrto is said to have visited Socrates on the morning of his death, on which occasion she behaved rudely to Xantippe, who, with her infant in her arms, had spent the night in prison to comfort her husband. Despite all this, Socrates is generally represented as a saintly character and his wife as a termagant.

The biblical account does not mention the name of Noah's wife nor her age. (The age of women is never given by biblical writers, except in the case of Sarah.) But she was no longer young at the time of the

Deluge, and it was no easy task for her to whack, drag and coax the animals into the Ark and to attend to the extermination of vermin, the disposal of garbage, the detection of stowaways, etc. Noah, on the other hand, belonged to the builders of the race, to the family of Columbus and Robinson Crusoe, the apolaustic type noted for arduous physical feats. Yet, he spent his time on board playing games of thoughtless agility (quoits and shuffle board) and performing on the kettledrum, on which he excelled in reproducing the mutterings of distant thunder and approaching storms, and also imposing silence on the crew during animal inspections and fire drills. In a more rejoicing mood he would play the Irish bagpipes, considered by those disposed to listen to them as the most melodious of all instruments. To be shut up with this quaint captain on a floating menagerie, with menacing waters without and a gray sky overhead, with no avenue of escape, surrounded by predatory carnivora, esurient bears, flatulent elephants and salacious camels, did little to contribute to the preservation of conjugal affection. We cannot read the early account of the Flood without admiring this anonymous morigerous heroine in her passage through a sea of domestic troubles.

IV

English, a Masculine Language?

THE THEORETICAL BASIS FOR THE DISPARAGEMENT OF ENGLISH IS FOUND in the so-called "degeneration theory," according to which a language becomes poorer the more it changes. Schopenhauer, who was a proponent of this theory, thus took Sanskrit to be the purest and English the most degenerate of all the languages. When English in the course of its development lost its inflectional endings, imported foreign words, unsexed its nouns and discarded the subjunctive mood together with other superfluous grammatical distinctions, it became in the eyes of its admirers (Adam Smith, Mallarmé, Walt Whitman, Otto Jespersen) a more efficient instrument of communication, gaining in force what it lost in formal elegance. A sword is not a better weapon for being embroidered and bejewelled. By dispensing with pedantic and antiquated grammatical rules the English succeeded in reforming their language on logical principles more congenial to the rational mind. To the detractors of our language, however, this lamentable development is not a sign of progress; to maintain that it contributed to greater conciseness and increased vigor is like saying that a man has gained in strength when his eyes have grown dim, his legs stiff and his ears deaf.

A conspicuous example of hostility to the English language is that of the Austrian poet, Rainer Maria Rilke, who was obsessed with an unrelenting aversion for all things English and, by extension, American. His deep-seated hatred of our language was not based on personal experience and independent judgment but on ready-made generalizations that were common in Germany in the early part of the century. Throughout his life the gifted poet affected total ignorance of the English language and openly encouraged this misleading impression, although he had translated Elizabeth Barret Browning's *Sonnets from the Portuguese* with great skill.

Another curious example of hatred of our language is provided by Louis Wolfson, the amazing American logophile. In his strange autobiography, written in French *(Le schizo et les langues, 1970),* he describes and analyzes his aversion for his mother tongue—which was a reflection of the schizophrenic hatred he bore to his mother. Every English word that she uttered in her piercing voice wounded him like a blow on the head. He finally conceived an ingenious plan to protect his ears against his mother's lingual aggression. As soon as her menacing words struck his ears, he destructured or defused them by employing complicated rules of phonological decomposition whereby he converted his mother's words into phonic equivalences found in other languages. Thus, when he heard the words "vegetable shortening," he decomposed them into foreign words denoting grease and fat: Ger. *schmalz,* Heb. *shemen,* Rus. *jir.* Or, on hearing the phrase: "Don't trip over the wire," he rapidly transformed it into: *Tu' n* icht (Ger.) *tré* bucher (Fr.) über (Ger.) *hé* (Heb. def. art.) *prov* olka (Rus. *vor* wire = *rov* backwards). The basic requirement in these linguistic transformations is *rapidity* of the process and the *conservation* of the sound and structure of the English word. The ultimate aim of this strange employment, if realized, would be to reunite all foreign languages into one continuous idiom: to redo what Babel undid.

Detractors of our language find evidence of its uncouth masculinity in the circumstance that it has been obliged to borrow from the French language words denoting psychological moods and refined manners, since the expression of delicate sentiments was in former times associated with French culture: *finesse, joie de vivre, blasé, sang froid, amour propre, faux pas* and *je ne sais quoi*. Evidence of our masculine ego is also found in the perpendicular English personal pronoun "I"—proud and domineering in its radical isolation as it raises its Self with singular abruptness to gratify its craving for recognition. We write this pretentious pronoun in English with a capital letter whereas *you* is written with a small letter, the reverse of German where *Du* and *Sie* are majuscule and *ich* minuscule; the latter is, moreover, internally related in both form and sound to its accusative *mich,* unlike the disequiparent *I-me,* thus permitting an eternal play of the Self with It-self, as elaborated in Fichte's philosophical system.

Further proof of masculine heartlessness is the paucity of endearing diminutives in our language (with corresponding feelings of tenderness), such as we find in profusion in Russian, Spanish and German—although not in Hebrew, which is obliged to borrow diminutive forms from the Yiddish. English "babyisms and dear diminutives" (Tennyson) sound frivolous and are for the most part restricted to the nursery (Dickie, auntie, tootsie-wootsie). The relatively few diminutives in our language are hardly recognized as such: pock*et* (dim. of *poke*), toil*et* (dim. of Fr. *toile* cloth), nozz*le* (little nose), thimb*le* (little thumb), crad*le* (little basket). On the other hand, English has few augmentatives compared to the Romance languages, and these for the most part are of foreign origin: ball*oon*, bass*oon*, tromb*one*, mill*ion*—a rare native augmentative being *spittoon.* If the paucity of diminutives in our language is taken to indicate the absence in its speakers of qualities of tenderness and modesty, then the lack of augmentatives should with equal cogency indicate the absence of braggadocio and gasconade.

Defenders of English perceive its masculine nature in the pronunciation of its consonant-clustered words, such as *months, wealth, feasts, fifth, twelfth, strength* (with its single vowel submerged by seven consonants). English words conflict with the principles of human articulation and can be produced only with the aid of facial distortions and grimaces.

One must be careful to pronounce English words as they are *not* written. Foreign mouths are not equipped to speak our language, and despair of its unpredictable pronunciation: *colonel, indict, impious, victuals, forecastle, boatswain, recipe;* place names: *Arkansas, Poughkeepsie, Sioux City, Houston, Worcester;* surnames: *Bagehot* (Bedjet), *Strachan* (Strawn), *St. Clair* (Sinclair), *Milnes* (Mills), *Vaughan* (Vorn). To foreign ears our language sounds like the humming through a comb and is often indistinguishable from the braying of an ass, e.g., the audible spelling of a word like *r-a-r-e-r* (ah, eh, ah, ee, ah). This inability of the English to lift the tongue to an erect position to produce the apical *r* sound (hampered by stiff upper lip and pipe) is a further incriminating symptom of weakened masculinity detected by unfriendly psychologists. English children and many adults often substitute an *l* for an *r* like the Chinese *(flied lice)* or pronounce it faintly *(wed wed wose).* We appear to be offended by the rolling uvular *r* (Fr. *grasseyer*) and have succeeded in removing this exciting sound from our language where it has given up all claim, except in Scotland, to the rank of a consonant.

Attempts have been made from time to time to preserve the masculine vigor of our native tongue, the least feeble of which was the so-called *"Anglosaxification movement"* of linguistic purification in England at the end of the last century. It counted among its members many distinguished literary figures, including Charles M. Doughty, the author of *Arabia Deserta,* the historian E. A. Freeman and the poet William Barnes, whose linguistic theories were seriously studied by Thomas Hardy and Gerard Manley Hopkins. The principal aim of this movement was to remove all words from our language that bore the bar sinister of foreign origin, chiefly French and Latin, and return to the "naked thew and sinew" of English, to the blunt Saxon words that reach the mind directly through the senses:

> The cat came fiddling out of the barn,
> With a bundle of bagpipes under his arm,
> Fiddle dee dee! Fiddle dee dee!
> The mouse has wedded the bumble bee.

The writers associated with this movement thus sought to replace words of foreign origin with more robust regional or archaic words: lunatic/moon-sick, neck/halse, pedestrian/foot-folk, muscle/brawn, sea/brine, music/gleecraft, arithmetic/rimecraft, etc. This zeal to purify the language by reviving obsolete words, together with stylistic peculiarities borrowed from the German, had a deplorable effect on our language. Many books were written in the style of these teutonizing philologists; but their efforts proved to be incompatible with the genius of the English language, and the Anglosaxification movement was soon abandoned. The revival of archaic or obsolete words continued to be a matter of debate, some critics regarding it as detrimental to the development of our language—"The man who writes in Saxon/ Is the man to use an ax on" (Ambrose Bierce)—while others thought it enhanced its vigor and expressiveness yet, in his *Notebook and Letters,* which is filled with words and phrases from the dialect of farmers and workers, Gerard Manley Hopkins wrote: "I am learning Anglosaxon, and it is vastly superior to what we have now. . . . it makes one weep to think what English might have been."

Obsolete Words or Verbal Dropouts

A word may always be found lurking in the background of a normal word, waiting to usurp its place when its vitality has weakened. Thus, in the Middle Ages adultery displaced *spouse-breach;* butcher, *flesher;* judge, *doomsman;* despair, *wanhope;* mask, *grima;* doctor, *leech;* sky, *lyft;* hostage, *gisl;* cemetery, *licburg;* dirge, *licsang* (from the first word in the Catholic service for the dead: *Dirige, domine,* direct, O Lord. . . . Ps. 5:9). Words are often discarded as the result of homonymic conflict. Words that sound alike are not likely to be confused when they are spelled differently or when they perform different functions in the sentence or are used in exclusive contexts, for example, the *fly* that buzzes and the *fly* of the trousers, the *pupil* of the eye and the *pupil* in the classroom (although both are under the lash). Where ambiguity occurs, however, one of the homonyms may be abandoned or displaced by another word.

Disease, originally a euphemism meaning "lack of ease," superseded OE *adl,* which went out of use because of its phonetic resemblance to OE *adela* mud, filth (but retained in *addle-egg,* a rotten egg that produces no chicks, and *addle-brained,* muddle-headed); *kidney* supplanted OE *near* (Ger. *Niere*) because *a near* conflicted with *an ear; queen* after a long struggle drove out *quean,* which at first simply meant "woman," but in ME acquired the meaning of "harlot," so that when the two words, at first phonetically distinct, came to be pronounced alike, the danger of confusing the wife or consort of the monarch with a harlot could no longer be ignored, and the coarser word *quean* was abandoned; OF *vair* a grayish fur (Eng. mini*ver*) and *verre* glass account for a glass slipper being erroneously substituted for Cinderella's fur slipper, a misunderstanding first pointed out by Balzac in 1836.

Homonymic conflict is a constant linguistic phenomenon. The word *sextet* is now being cautiously used in musical circles until a less compromising substitute is found; *succour* has practically disappeared since its phonetic resemblance to *sucker* can lead to an embarrassing ambiguity, as in the case of the English clergyman who during the last war thanked the Lord for the "American succour."

A word becomes obsolete when the thing it denotes ceases to exist or when the custom it describes is no longer observed, for example:

CODPIECE, also codpiss, a conspicuous bagged appendage inserted in front of close-fitting breeches worn by men from the fifteenth to the seventeenth century, designed for extravagant penile display and assertion of phallic prowess; excellent reproductions of this audacious piece of clothing appear in Holbein's portrait of Henry VIII, *The Pride of Life,* and in Luca Signorelli's fresco, *The End of the World.* A less modest appendage, known as *braguette,* was worn beneath a short coat, clearly outlining the male genitals.

CORSNED, a piece of bread or cheese about an ounce in weight which an accused person was required to swallow; if it stuck in the throat, causing paleness and convulsions, the accused was pronounced guilty.

GEMONIES, the steps leading to the Tiber to which the bodies of condemned criminals were dragged and thrown into the river.

INGLE, or ningle, a boy-favorite, a catamite; *to ningle,* to wantonly dally with boys against nature. The origin of this word, given in all dictionaries as "unknown," may well be the Yiddish *yingel,* young boy.

RANDLE, a customary form of punishment which compelled Irish schoolboys to recite a nonsensical poem as an apology for farting in front of a schoolmate.

SERGEANTRY, the personal service rendered to English kings in lieu of rent. This included a dance performed before the king on Christmas day, consisting of a saltus, a sufflatus and a bumbulus, accompanied by a noise made with puffed cheeks (a Bronx cheer?) and ending with a rousing fart, for such was the jolly mirth of royalty in the days of merry England.

SKIMINGTON, a burlesque procession or charivari of discordant noises (Ital. *scampanati,* Ger. *Katzenmusik*), designed to annoy or insult unpopular newlyweds or to ridicule a henpecked husband or shrewish wife; cf. Hogarth's engraving, *Hudibras and Skimington,* which depicts a disorderly skimington mob.

Many common objects familiar to us from the days of our childhood are gone and almost entirely forgotten: smithies, free-lunch counters, cigar-store Indians, hat pins, collar buttons, inkwells, spittoons. It is useless to deplore their loss. Now and then they will be recalled with feelings of nostalgia, for they evoke memories of happier days. Obsolete words, however, are not entirely lost. They are preserved in our dictionaries, the cemeteries of forgotten words, where they constitute more than one-fifth of the total number (ca. 85,000) and where, marked obsolete or archaic, they silently await resurrection. Some have been revived and brought back into use after many centuries, such as *bigot* and *smolder;* others were taken from dialects and given wider currency: *ornery,* a contracted form of "ordinary," *gallivant,* an elaboration of "gallant," *pernickety,* an echoic expansion of "particular." Sir Walter Scott rescued from oblivion *glee, gruesome, glamor, weird,* and *stalwart;* and Robert Burns before him, *eerie, uncanny* and *gloaming.* Students of Mark Twain have counted 743 archaisms in his works, among them *malison,* a doublet of "malediction"; *donjon,* a doublet of "dungeon"; *doxy,* an unmarried mistress of a beggar or rogue. Many words considered obsolete in the eighteenth century are now in common use: *baleful, beverage, fray, langorous, murky, ruination, unkempt.* Other obsolete or regional words will doubtlessly be restored from time to time. Many of them should never have been allowed to die, such as:

BEDSWERVER, an unfaithful spouse; FIFISH, foolish (at first applied to people from the county of Fife in Scotland); HAME-SUCKEN, the crime of assaulting a person in his own house; MANAVELINS, scraps of food, odds and ends; SPHAIRISTIC, pertaining to the game of tennis; STORGE, the affection of parents for their offspring; SWINK, to toil (past tense: swonk); YULY, beautiful. Especially regrettable is the loss of a number of obsolete onomapoetic words which formerly invigorated our lethargic speech: CHEHO, to sneeze; CLOOP, the sound made on removing the cork from the bottle; GRANCH, to gnash the teeth; HATCH, to cough; YEX, to hiccup (past tense: yox); TWEEDLE, the sound of a violin, adopted by John Byrom, an eighteenth-century author of religious verse in coining the phrase "Tweedledum and Tweedle-dee."

From a rationalistic point of view, progress in language is measured by its ability to assemble diverse aspects of an object or activity under one comprehensive notion as a unifying principle. A language is said to advance when it is able to liberate its words from their parochial attachments to a particular culture and subsume them under universal logical principles inherent in the human mind. Antirationalists, on the other hand, regard a language as impoverished when it obscures the concrete, sensible aspects of a word and erases meaningful distinctions: the bricks of a chimney are not the same as those of a church, and the wood in a "heart of oak" not the same as that in a "head of oak." A language is richer for resisting excessive abstraction and retaining its concrete forms, as for example the various words in Hebrew for "removing" or "taking off," depending on whether one takes off a garment, hat, shoes, wig, veil, armor, phylacteries, eyeglasses, (amputated) leg, dust from an object, fruit from a tree.

Each language makes its own distinctions for which it creates separate words. English makes distinctions probably not found in other languages: flesh/meat, tall/high, shadow/shade, sex/gender, bunions/corns, egoist/egotist, naked/nude, old/ancient, chorus/choir, alien/foreigner, slander/libel, freedom/liberty.[1] On the other hand, English makes no distinction between the body as a living organism and as physical matter (Ger. *Leib, Körper*), the heart as an organ of the body and as the seat of the emotions (Arab. *kalb, fuad*), death of a man and that of an animal (Ger. *sterben, kreppieren;* Heb. *met, peger*), the kick of a man and the kick of a horse (Fr. *coup de pied, ruade*), words in isolation and words in a meaningful context (Ger. *Wörter, Worte*), a word as the bearer of meaning as opposed to its mere physical structure (Heb. *milah, teva*), the crust of a loaf of bread and its soft part (Fr. *la croute, la mie*), playing a game and playing an instrument (Span. *jugar, tocar*), the corner of a room and the corner of a street (Span. *rincón, esquina*), the heel of the foot, the shoe and the boot (Ger. *Ferse, Absatz, Hacken*), dark blue and sky blue (Rus. *sini, golibu*), black as color and black as darkness (Navaho Indian), pale yellow as the hue

---

[1]Liberty is a political ideal; freedom is a more personal concept referring to the restraints of our general human condition and not only to its political aspects. German, French and Russian have one word for the two concepts *(Freiheit, liberté, svoboda);* Hebrew has three.

of straw or cloth and as the color of ripening bananas or leaves (Zuni Indian).

Philosophical Distinctions

Latin makes a distinction between visible and invisible light *(lux, lumen)* and between the two meanings of "outside" *(praeter, extra)*, that which is outside the mind but attainable in theory, and that which is unattainable because it is beyond consciousness. The two forms of the Spanish verb "to be" *(ser, estar)* express a subtle distinction: *Soy, más estoy*/I am and what's more I am here now—a valuable existential distinction. The two words in German for "historical" *(historisch, geschichtlich)* can serve in theological studies to distinguish between Jesus as a category of the unique (divine) and as the subject of historical investigation. A convenient distinction is made in Russian between two conceptions of truth *(istinna, pravda)*, the abstract notion of truth common to all men, and truth that is realizable in a specific social context and hence the common goal of social morality. Greek has two words for "flesh" *(sarx, soma)* as over against the Hebrew *basar*, a distinction that plays an important part in Pauline theology; two words for "time" *(chronos, kairos)*, passing or wasting time, and time charged with moments of intensity, turning points; two words for "word" *(epos, logos)*, the word as incantation, associated with song, and the word as the bearer of reflective thought. Greek also has three words for "cause": *aitía* motive force, *prophasis* excuse or reason, and *arché* beginning or origin (Ger. *Ursache*).

Despite our extensive vocabulary—the *Oxford New English Dictionary* consists of twelve volumes weighing 200 pounds, containing 414,825 words that cover a period of twelve centuries and 178 miles of type—we lack many words that may be found in other languages. Restricting our examples to words pertaining to parts and functions of the body alone, we have no word to denote hair that grows at the back of the neck (Ital. *zazzera*) or between the eyebrows (Fr. *taroupe*), baldness at the temples (Ger. *Geheimratsecken* or *Ehestandswinkeln*), the space between the outstretched thumb and the forefinger (Arab. *fitr*),

the fleshy part of the palm below the thumb (Ger. *die Maus*), a woman
with a not unpleasing mustache (Ital. *baffona*), the groaning and strain-
ing that accompany defecation (Rum. *escreme*). We also have no word
for the space between the fingernail and the flesh where dirt collects
(Pers.), the cavity behind the ear (Hindi), the hollow between the
lower lip and the chin (Gr.), one of the legs of a pair of trousers (Urdu),
the rapid and repeated breaking of wind (Akkad.), one who wears his
trousers loose at the waist and is in constant fear of losing them (Ital.),
the genital orifice of a female animal (Kurdish), the repeated clearing
and blowing of the nose (Korean), the slight shudder experienced
immediately after urination (Span.).

A gap in our language that is particularly hard to swallow concerns
our paltry vocabulary in the matter of drinking, an activity in which
we profess to be second to none. The few words we have refer to
greedy drinking: swig, swill, quaff and guzzle (in Scotland food as well
can be guzzled). The one drink that can be called purely American, as
Mark Twain observed, is ice water, a national habit no foreigner can
understand. Our language is weak in bibulous terminology. Some
words we once had have not survived: *cloop*, coined by Thackeray to
render the noise a cork makes when leaving the bottle; *supernacular* to
describe an excellent wine is a modern Latin rendering of the German
auf den Nagel trinken, the practice of turning up an emptied glass on
the left thumbnail to show that all the liquor has been drunk to the
last drop. In this highly contested area of drinking the Italians, to judge
from their drinking vocabulary, reign supreme: *bere a sciacquabudella,*
to drink on an empty stomach; *bere grosso,* to drink a wine appropriate
to the character of the food; *bere a garganilla,* pouring a drink down
the throat into the open mouth without touching the vessel with the
lips; as well as words to describe the mark left on the tablecloth by a
wet glass *(culaccino)* or the humming sound made by the finger running
along the rim of the glass *(ziro-ziro),* and words to indicate when glasses
are to be filled, emptied and replenished.

Words to Describe Natural Sounds

The English language is poor in words to describe natural sounds. We have no word to render the sound of water being poured out in great quantities (Fr. *glouglou*, Ger. *Gluckgluck*), the rapid eating of raw vegetables or the chattering of storks (as in Turkish). Nor do we have words for the different kinds of sneezes: the spluttering, the explosive, the apologetic and the stifled—and here again the palm must be awarded to the Turks. With respect to words to describe the various eructations and demonic winds that proceed from the inferior part of the human frame, the Persian language is without rival: the hesitant, the subdued, the flippant and discordant, the unclouded and deflated, the inevitable and triumphant. The sound of breaking wind, when called for on the English stage, is made respectable in conformity with British censorship by having a bass trombone in the wings play the Destiny Theme from Beethoven's Fifth Symphony. The sound of this wind instrument is associated with the color of yellow and is reputed to have a corporeal effect on listeners, often to a point of vulgarity.

The weakness of our language in describing the different noises that reach the human ear has compelled writers to rely on their own linguistic inventions to render in printed symbols the natural sounds they hear around them. A well-known example that attempts to render the deafening uproar of a cataract is to be found in Robert Southey's poem "The Cataract of Lodore" (towards the end). At the beginning of *Finnegan's Wake*, Joyce describes the sound of thunder with a word of more than one hundred letters. Joyce is responsible for the following ingenious onomapoetic words, although none has as yet found its way into the dictionary:

> *Animal sounds:* the meow of a cat, *mrkgnai;* the bleating of a goat, *megegaggegg;* the neigh of a horse, *hohohohohohoh!*
> *Inanimate objects:* a snapping button, *bip;* a tired gasjet, *pwfungg;* the rattle of a pebble, *rtststr;* dirty water going down the hole of a lavatory sink, *suck* (only much louder); a blind man tapping with a stick, *tap tap tap* (in the French translation: *toc toc toc*).

Sounds that proceed from the human body: the sound of a yawn, *Iiiiiiiiaaaaaaach;* the sound of a sneeze, *pcho* (abortive), *whooshe* or *housit* (effusive); the sound of borborgym (a rumbling in the bowels accompanied by intestinal gas discharges), *Pff. OO. Rrps. Pprrpffrrppfff.* The groans, grunts and ejaculations that accompanied the fornication of Blazes and Molly were heard by Joyce and unflinchingly transcribed by him on paper as follows:

He: Ah! Gooblazeqrukbrukarchkrasht!

She: OO! Weeshwashtkissmapooisthnapoochuck!

The French edition of *Ulysees,* in which Joyce himself participated, renders these exclamations as:

He: Hah! Bondacheerokbrutarchkracht!

She: Hoh! Ouissouassbizimapoothnapoojoui!

And these appear in the German version, for those who are interested in subtle national differences, as:

He: Ah! Gublasruckbrukrachkrasch!

She: Oh! Wiwawuschküssichbiarisnaarfuck!

We can for the time being dispense with many foreign words for which we have no equivalent in English, however useful they may be in their respective cultures. The things they represent may be pointed to without being dignified with a specific name; or they may be referred to by some whimsical term, such as doodad, thingamabob or watchamacallit. English consists of thousands of words borrowed from every language under the sun, and we may profitably borrow (pilfer) many more, by force if necessary, such as:

ITALIAN: *frontespiziaio,* one whose knowledge of books does not extend beyond the frontispiece or title page; *zuzzeralone,* a grown-up man who takes delight in childish games, a boy at heart.

SPANISH: *desasnar,* lit. to unass (someone), to teach a boor manners; *ensimismarse,* to find a place within one's inner self from which one can view the world with equanimity (Ger. *insichselbst* versenken).

FRENCH: *esprit d'escalier* (Ger. *Treppenwitz*), a brilliant retort that occurs to one as an afterthought on the staircase after leaving, and one which in time one believes to have actually been made, much like a physician who finds an infallible remedy after the patient is dead. (Such retorts and bon-mots have been collected and published, cf. *Treppenwitz der Weltgeschichte.*)

RUSSIAN: *prijivalshchik,* a friend or relative who comes for a visit, stays on indefinitely, constantly complaining about the food, arrangements, etc; *skloka* refers to the petty intrigues, secret hostilities, scheming and spying that go on in a totalitarian society in which people are constrained to conceal their real thoughts.

CZECH: *litost* stands for feelings of hostility, remorse and self-pity directed chiefly against one's self, a condition that is widespread in a country where people who are dissatisfied with their lot are condemned to repress their feelings of envy and guilt.

SWAHILI: *zuzua,* to praise a person in fun until he believes the compliments showered upon him and as a result acquires an unwarranted high opinion of his qualities, leading him to behave foolishly.

GERMAN: *Geltungsbedürfnis,* the psychological need for self-assertion, the need to be in the limelight; *Ohrfeigengesicht,* a cheeky, impudent face that invites a slap (Fr. *tête à gifle*); *Zechpreller,* one who evades paying the bill in a restaurant or tavern by hasty departure; *Lobhudelei,* back-slapping mutual admiration, especially by members of the same fraternity, profession, etc.; *Zaungast,* one who contemplates the human scene (skeptically) and not as a suffering participant.

HEBREW: *teku,* questions for which there are no answers; *tatranut* (the last word in the Hebrew dictionary), a defective sense of smell—an affliction from which Gandhi suffered, but by no means a misfortune in India.

The opaqueness and impenetrability of English words may be the chief sign of English masculinity. Our language contains a large number of so-called "learned or bookish words," mostly derived from Latin and Greek, words that are not likely to be understood even by the educated native without consulting a large dictionary:

> *borborite,* one who holds immoral doctrines and indulges in obscene talk; *borborygm,* a rumbling in the bowels; *brolliology,* the study of umbrellas; *crepedarian,* relating to a shoemaker; *exergue,* part of the reverse side of a coin below the main device, often filled in by the date, etc.; *genial* (when accented on the second syllable), relating to the chin; *gremial,* a silken apron placed on the bishop's lap to keep his vestments clean from oil when celebrating Mass or conferring orders; *kakopraxian,* refering to the habit of picking one's nose, after kakopraxis, the ill-mannered guest who idly picked his nose at Zeus's table; *novercal,* relating to, or characteristic of, a stepmother; *onolatry,* the adulation of the lowly ass; *opisthography,* the writing on both sides of a sheet of paper; *opsimathy,* learning that is acquired late in life; *pandurate,* shaped like a fiddle; *retromingent,* urinating backwards, also an animal that does so, e.g., a camel.

But even ordinary English words in daily use are inscrutable to the native speaker with respect to their origin and composition, typical English words without a discernible ancestry, progeny or living relations: *average, baffle, farce, fluke, hygiene, miscellaneous, puny, rehearsal, somersault, tiny, vanilla, rowdy, wiseacre.* The impenetrability of English words becomes evident when compared to their transparent German equivalents:

> constipated, *verstopft* stopped up; curfew, *Ausgehverbot* going-out-prohibition; halitosis, *Mundgeruch* mouth odor; iambic pentameter, *Fünffüssler* five-footer; pew, *Kirchenstuhl* church-stool; quadruped, *Vierfüssler* four-footer; skunk, *Stinktier* stink animal; thimble, *Fingerhut* finger hat.

A clear example of an opaque English word is *glove,* a solitary monosyllable of obscure origin (Goth. *lofa* hand, or Scot. *loof* palm of the hand?), with its gummy *g,* slippery *l,* hollow *o,* unmusical *v* and secretive *e*—wherein hostile critics profess to see a reflection of the enigmatic workings of the English mind. The word's sonic and graphic density holds meaning in abeyance and compels the mind to seek exploratory solutions through trial and error, as a sculptor chipping away stone is suddenly surprised by the emerging figure. The transparent Ger. *Handschuh* glove (lit. hand-shoe), on the other hand, reveals its meaning at first sight with a minimum of displacement between itself and its designation. It hastens the mind forward to meaning, and arrives too soon at its destination. It extinguishes itself, like a match, in the process of lighting up its object. This self-effacing, morigerous allegiance of the German word to its designation has made the German language, in the eyes of its speakers, "the heroic language par excellence" (Vico), but also a fertile source of mischief, isolating it from the philosophical tradition of the West and raising false expectations of national felicity to the detriment of generic humanity.

It is therefore a mistake on the part of philanthropic educators to remove or simplify obscure passages in school texts in their misdirected zeal for clarity. Noncomprehension is a prerequisite of knowledge and once dispelled cannot be easily restored. Logical clarity and precise formulation may even be an impediment in prayer and poetry, which are often more impressive when only imperfectly understood. Vernon Lee, for example, has analyzed the greatly admired description of the night scene in Walter Pater's classical study *Marius,* removing all its logical absurdities and errors of style. The rewritten version achieved clarity and consistency at the cost, however, of personal style, rhythmic patterns and glorious sounds. Similarly, Robert Graves is not to be applauded for indicating the incongruities and ill-chosen words in what is considered a great American masterpiece, revered and memorized by generations of school children, Lincoln's "Gettysburg Address," and rewriting it in plain, comprehensible English, as follows:

Some ninety years ago a noble group of American patriots—our forefathers—chosen spokesmen of thirteen colonies, signed and published a Declaration of Independence, still the prime charter of our Liberties. They protested to a tyrannical king that, having been born free, they were entitled to equal rights not only with his other subjects but with all free men everywhere. This challenge was taken up by their British oppressors and, in the bitter war for freedom that ensued, each former colony played its heroic part. A new Nation had come into being, a Union presently confirmed by a Constitutional treaty of independent states, bound together in loyalty under a central guiding power directed by their own chosen President. . . .

(*The Crane Bag and Other Disputed Subjects,* Chap. 18)

The following passage from Ecclesiastes was rewritten by George Orwell in the jargon of contemporary sociology as a warning to those who are tempted to make classical literature more comprehensible to the modern reader:

I returned, and saw under the sun, that the race is not to the swift, nor the battle to the strong, neither yet bread to the wise, nor yet riches to men of understanding, nor yet favour to men of skill, but time and chance happeneth to them all.

Objective consideration of contemporary phenomena compels the conclusion that success or failure in competitive activities exhibits no tendency to be commensurate with innate capacity, but that a considerable element of the unpredictable must invariably be taken into account.

(Quoted from Arthur Koestler, *Act of Creation,* London, 1964, p. 323)

V

The Role of the Mother Tongue

THE WIDESPREAD BELIEF IN THE INADEQUACY OF HUMAN REASON, THE
distinctive theme of modern life preached by its most eminent critics,
Rousseau, Nietzsche, Carlyle, Bergson, William James and D.H. Lawrence, among others, entailed grave consequences for the historical
destiny of Western philosophical thought. Reason dethroned was at
different times usurped by the rebel forces of race and blood (Nietzsche), an all-powerful state (Hegel), early Nordic myths (Wagner),
economic determinism (Karl Marx), or the new deity of historicism,
the belief in historical destiny and national mission. In the early part
of the last century in Germany it was the national tongue that laid claim
to the throne left vacant by Reason in accordance with the shift of
sovereignty in the intellectual world of that day from *ratio* to *oratio*,
from the rational forms of universal grammar revealed to the eye to
the sounds of colloquial speech perceived by the ear and organized into
the social patterns of the mother tongue.

This fateful change in thought and feeling was the work of a number of influential writers and thinkers of the last century, mostly German, who taught that society is a living organism (Herder) possessing a collective mind and a will of its own (Durkheim) reflected in the mother tongue, the repository of its beliefs and myths (Grimm) and incorporated in the constitution of the state and its laws (Savigny), this being the principal bond of national unity (Fichte). Each language has a definite spiritual task allotted to it by Providence (Mazzini), and it is the "heroic" German language, uncontaminated by foreign admixture, that has the sacred mission of redeeming mankind (Vico).

The patriotic love of one's native or adopted land and its speech is not inconsistent with feelings of universalism. The Psalmist sat down by the waters of Babylon and wept for Jerusalem. Lord Byron longed for Italy, for "the fount at which the panting Mind assuages/ Her thirst for knowledge," as did Browning: "Open my heart and you will see/ Graved inside of it 'Italy' "; Kipling loved one fair spot in his native land above all others, Sussex by the sea:

> God gives all men all earth to love,
>   But, since man's heart is small,
> Ordains for each one spot shall prove
>   Belovèd over all.
> Each to his choice, and I rejoice
>   The lot has fallen to me
> In a fair ground—in a fair ground—
>   Yea, Sussex by the sea!

Nothing is dearer to us than our native home and the sound of its speech. The pangs of exile of the hopelessly damned in the *Divine Comedy* were for a brief moment relieved when they were permitted to hear the sweet accents of their Tuscan dialect. No greater calamity can befall a man than to leave his homeland and be compelled to learn a foreign tongue: Fr. *depaysé*, literally "to be out of one's country," came to mean "to be uprooted, bewildered." Mowbray in *King Richard II*, banished from the kingdom and condemned to live abroad, bemoans above all else the loss of his native speech:

The language I have learnt these forty years,
My native English, now I must forgo,
And now my tongue's use is to me no more
Than an unstringed viol or a harp,
Or like a cunning instrument cas'd up—
Or being open, put into his hands
That knows no touch to tune the harmony.
Within my mouth you have engaol'd my tongue,
Doubly portcullis'd with my teeth and lips,
And dull unfeeling barren ignorance
Is made my gaoler to attend on me.
I am too old to fawn upon a nurse,
Too far in years to be a pupil now:
What is thy sentence then but speechless death,
Which robs my tongue from breathing native breath?

Before the end of the century, however, this innocent love of one's country began its fatal movement into the realm of Nordic mythology with its tribal metaphors of blood, race, soil and Aryan superiority. The nation was now regarded as a living organism whose roots had to be nourished by life-giving myths embedded in the mother tongue. Rival languages were frowned upon and even suppressed in the interest of national unity. In one of his poems, called "To a German," Herder reproves a youth who greets his mother in French on returning home from abroad and urges him "to spew out the ugly slime of the Seine and speak German." The stranger who does not speak the native tongue is mistrusted, for we have no means of deciphering his unexpressed thoughts and have no access to his mind:

The Stranger within my gate,
  He may be true or kind,
But he does not talk my talk—
  I cannot feel his mind.
I see the face and the eyes and the mouth,
  But not the soul behind.
                                    —Thomas Hardy

Political boundaries were made to coincide with linguistic boundaries. The study of philology became a branch of anthropology and an instrument of politics. The German language, and not the shape of the skull, was now the mark and criterion of nationhood. One who spoke German was a German, literally by paying lip-service (except a Jew).[1]

We live in different worlds when we speak different languages. There is no universal grammar, no universal conscience or code of morality. The sole basis of human unification is to be found neither in religious beliefs, political affiliation nor social classes, but in a common language, the mother tongue in which the visible world is revealed to us. The balm of folk-poetry heals the wounds inflicted by the cold intellect. This emphasis on the national tongue was the German answer to the French Revolution, which had made abstract reason the indispensable instrument of cognition and the principal guide to political action.

Since the national character is reflected in language, it follows that the true character of a people can be studied in the structure of its speech, in its vocabulary and idioms, its intuitive images and etymological coincidences. A voluminous literature, for the most part anecdotal, has grown up around this dubious assumption. The refined nasality of French speech, for example, is said to reflect the rationalistic cast of the French mind; the frequency of the *e* vowel, the serenity of the Gallic spirit and its fine sense of proportion. The Spanish sense of realism is apparent in the use of the double accusative *(verle a Ud.),* its conservatism in the common phrase *sin novedad* (nothing new), its stoical indifference in *no importa* (no matter, never mind). The Russian dislike of monotony is evident in the shifting accent of Russian words that

---

[1]The Jews, according to Hegel, are by their nature and history sworn enemies of the State and have no allegiance to a fatherland, so that no rational society can tolerate them for long. This German theory of language as an instrument of politics and form of nationhood reappears (in a less arrogant manner) in the struggle between Yiddish and Hebrew after the establishment of the state of Israel, Yiddish being defended as the expression of the Jewish collective soul, Hebrew being defended as the bond of national unity and criterion of political identity and common origin.

moves backward and forward from syllable to syllable; the Russian penchant for the tawdry and tasteless is seen in the common word *poshlust,* although this would seem to be more typical of the German spirit *(Kitsch, Talmi).* The German use of the past perfect as an imperative form *(aufgestanden!* stand up) is taken as evidence of the nation's militaristic spirit; its throaty sounds, which make heavy demands on the inner man, indicate the philosophic depth (obscurity) of the German mind; and the word *Schadenfreude,* a gloating over the misery of others, denotes a typical German trait, although the Greeks also have a word for it, ἐπιχαιρκακια, introduced into Latin by Cicero as *malevolentia.* Additional evidence of Teutonic insensitivity is found in the circumstance that, although the German language has a word to denote the back of the hand *(Handrücke)* with which to strike and slap, it has no word for the palm of the hand that is used to caress, beg and implore.

We find an unreflective predilection in various cultures for different parts of the body. The Spaniards emphasize the (shrugging) shoulders, the national gesture of indifference and procrastination; the French, the (slobbering) lips, indicating a highly developed stage of oral eroticism;[2] the Persians, the (erogenous) cavity behind the ear; the Americans, the balls of the feet and the (protruding) chin, the stance of the salesman, the American type par excellence. The Eskimos hold the thumb in

---

[2]An infallible way to recognize a Frenchman, apart from his passion for food and wine, is by his facial expression when talking, for the French language contains more lip-rounding vowels than any other, and even its consonants bring the tongue farther forward, giving the French face (in British eyes) a brazen, untrustworthy look. The French have no word for "blushing" *(rougir,* to grow red, does not distinguish between "blush" and "flush"). The English nebulous vowels and hard consonants beneath the proverbial stiff upper lip account for the drearier faces of the English.

Blushing seems to be a nineteenth-century English phenomenon and is often found in the works of Darwin, Burke, Dickens, Jane Austen and Meredith. among others. It is no longer in fashion among the young, who have nothing to conceal, "letting it all hang out." The French are not easily flustered *(je-m'en-foutisme),* and it is from them that we have had to borrow words that conceal embarrassment—nonchalant, blasé, sangfroid, insouciant, debonair—words that are not easily pronounced by us and should perhaps be returned to the French together with fiancé, dégagé, fracas, déjà vu and avoirdupois.

reverence as the most precious part of the human body, the part from which (in Eskimo folklore) God created Eve. Chinese life and thought revolve around the belly, which is regarded as the seat of learning and wisdom. The Russians hold on to the nose, an obvious phallic symbol that keeps turning up in Russian proverbs, idioms, surnames and even in dreams (the Russian word for dream *son* is nose *nos* reversed). In Hebrew literature the most significant part of the body is the face *panim,* not the masked Chinese "face" that can be lost and saved, but the face as the visible reflection of the inner life of the spirit.

No impartial observer of national character could fail to note that the German emphasis falls preponderately on the (protuberant) buttocks and (open) bowels. The ancient Greeks, as is commonly known, entertained a high notion of the human backside, which they endowed with dignity and esthetic appeal: the epithet callipygous (*kallos* beauty, *pyge* buttocks) was applied to Aphrodite, the goddess of love.[3] The Germans, however, stress the sewage aspect of this part of the body associated in German life with the prestige of the latrine. An ancient saying has it that "the Teutons were born coming out of Pilate's fundament" *(Teutonici sunt nati venerunt de culo Pilati).* The anal region occupies an ambiguous place in German thinking. It is not only "the seat of castigation" (Luther), the seat of learning and scholarship (*Sitz-fleisch* assiduity) but also the part of the anatomy invoked in friendly altercation (the famous Götz-zitat) and affectionately known as *Popo,* an infantile reduplication of Lat. *podex* rump. This anatomical preference has been related to the buhlish structure of the German sentence with its stringy clauses in the form of sausages, *salsicia farta,* the German form *par excellence,* and also to the more calamitous *Zerstörungswut (furor teutonicus)* that breaks out from time to time and rages against a hostile world.

A conspicuous example of this national interest in the lower part of

---

[3] The statue of Aphrodite Kallipygos admiring her beautiful backside, and also the statue of Satyr admiring his, may be seen in John Onians, *Art and Thought in the Hellenistic Age,* London, 1979, p. 56.

the human frame is provided by Martin Luther, a man of windy digestion who was obsessed with an anal terror of the world which he regarded, as he himself puts it, as "one big asshole" (identified by the Irish as St. Patrick's Hole, believed to be the gateway to Purgatory). The inspiration for his solifidian doctrine, according to which man is saved by faith alone, came to Luther while he was sitting in the cloaca of the Tower, to which he would often repair to seek relief in his recurrent spiritual crises. This so-called *Turmerlebnis* (1518) has been omitted in the more recent biographies of the father of Protestantism, for no doctrine is enhanced nor its author flattered by being associated with the toilet. The medieval Church, however, was reconciled to this association, knowing that the life of the spirit is but a feeble thing without the sensuous substratum of gross matter: *super cloacam ecclesia.* Incense was used not only to mitigate the unpleasant odor of sulpher and brimstone (the Church being a favorite haunt of the devil) but also to protect the bishop's nostrils from the stench of the faithful around him, for this could not have been a sweet-smelling effluvia when we consider the unhygienic habits of the worshipers in those days when cleanliness was not next to godliness and "the purity of the body and its garments meant the impurity of the soul" (Paul).

Those who distrust the power of human reason to illumine reality counsel us to dispense with wordless logical thought and rely on the wisdom embedded in the hidden meanings and allusions of our mother tongue. People who speak before they think are often surprised at what they hear. Many a simple soul has acquired a reputation for deep thought and impressive speech merely by repeating common maxims and quotable platitudes with an air of epigrammatic novelty, especially if he is fortunate enough to have French or Yiddish as his mother tongue. English requires an added moment of inspiration.

Do not think first and then speak! Speak, and ideas will follow of themselves, just as footprints appear while walking.[4] Speak of an angel

---

[4]This is the burden of Heinrich von Kleist's brief but highly influential essay, "On the Completion of Thought While Speaking," written at the end of the eighteenth century.

and you will hear the rustling of his (!) wings. Do not strain after novel forms of expression: "Rote words are right words" (Joyce). This is contrary to what we have always been taught, namely, to think before we speak, to form concepts in our mind before we clothe them in words: *Reme tene, verba sequentur* | Seize the subject and the words will follow (Cato). Whatever we wish to say can be said *in principle*. If we fail to express ourselves properly, it is only because our ideas are confused. Quick comprehension is suspect. Human response requires delay, unlike that of animals who can only convey instruction and not information that is subject to interpretation. Instant understanding is at times undesirable, even fatal. Poems and prayers, for example, must be able to resist immediate transformation into meaning and to this end employ archaic words, ambiguity and various deliberately contrived visual and auditive obstacles as a kind of delaying tactic to detain the mind from arriving too soon at the meaning, just as a traveler might come upon a clearing only after a weary journey in a dark forest. It is best to leave our intentions inexplicit, to linger on dark passages and anacolutha and, on occasion, choose to be silent.

Those who advise us to speak before thinking also add that we do so quickly before the internal censor is alarmed and thinking begins to intrude. Between heart and lips there is a distorting mechanism that turns things into their opposites, so that the slightest hesitation permits the mind to bribe the corruptible heart with contrary thoughts (rationalizations). In his autobiography Stendhal confesses that he wrote better when he began a sentence not knowing how it would end. The method he devised for avoiding untruths was to write down past events immediately without rereading, revising or correcting what he had written. It was better to have a poor style, he declared, than to strike a theatrical pose for posterity, the disease to which French writers are particularly exposed. This principle of speaking quickly, familiar to students of Zen philosophy, is also recommended by Mark Twain in *What Is Man?:*

> When your mind is racing along from subject to subject and strikes an inspiring one, open your mouth and begin talking upon that matter—or take your pen and use that. It will interest your mind and concentrate it,

and it will pursue the subject with satisfaction. It will take full charge, and furnish the words itself. . . .

Well, take a "flash of wit"—repartee. Flash is the right word. It is out instantly. There is no time to arrange the words. There is no thinking, no reflecting. Where there is a wit-mechanism it is automatic in its action and needs no help. Where the wit-mechanism is lacking, no amount of study and reflection can manufacture the product.

The very sound of the words of the mother tongue can stimulate thought apart from the meanings they convey. The sound of a word is often more vital to the poet than the thing it represents: "The word *ivory* shines in the brain clear and brighter than any ivory seen from the mottled tusks of elephants" (Joyce). Wordsworth would have hesitated to compose a poem about the daffodil had that flower been called by a less agreeable name, for example, Ital. *tromboncino* little trumpet.[5] Writers have expressed a strong preference or aversion for the *sound* of a word. Keats loved the sound of *drowsy;* Thomas Hardy, *pale* and *phantom;* Joyce, *smithereens* and Ger. *Leib* body. Balzac heard the crackling of silk paper in the Fr. *fafiot* banknote; and to Leibniz's ear the Ger. *Geige* fiddle (related to Eng. *jig*) was the true rendering of the tune of that instrument. A French writer took the Hebrew word

---

[5] A re-examination of this familiar poem by psychoanalysts reveals that it was not the sound but the shape of the flower that inspired the poet's exhibitionist fancy as he lay on his couch "in vacant or pensive mood . . . and could not but be gay," dreaming of his dance with the wild daffodils. The flower's upright stem represented to his subconscious mind the male principle, and the horizontal trumpet the female principle, both being inseparable but related in a way that prevents the phallic stem from entering the vaginal trumpet—in short, a perfect reflection of the incest taboo that created a barrier between the poet and his sister. This interpretation is but one of the many vindictive attempts of psychoanalysts to reduce genius to pathology and neuroticize its masterpieces. Thus, Goethe's *Sorcerer's Apprentice* reveals the author's unconscious bedwetting; Wagner's *The Flying Dutchman* masturbatory tendencies; the heroic conceptions of Michelangelo, compulsive onanism, etc.

The habit of reducing moral and artistic traits to psychopathic origins was called "the bugaboo of morbid origin" by William James. Thus, Carlyle's pessimism was traced to his indigestion, Disraeli's garrulousness to his flatulence, Calvin's moral rigorism to his frustrated gluttony, Marx's untidy appearance to chronic constipation.

umlala (disaster) to be the most beautiful word he had ever heard. Ruskin tells us in his *Flors Clavigera* that as a child he was frightened by the word *crocodile*. Thomas Hood detested the sound of *charity;* De Quincy, *quibbling;* George Eliot, *crudity;* Joyce, *simony;* and Coleridge, the Ger. *Tod* death, which reminded him of a loathsome toad. The Ger. *Weib* (woman) was for Samuel Beckett "a flat, flabby, pasty kind of a word, all breasts and buttocks . . . a hell of a fine word." On Swift's lips *bowels* stood for all that was objectionable and distasteful. Walter Pater's favorite words were *morsel, quaint, winsome* and *debonair;* and those of Mark Twain, *orgy, high-tone* and *blatherskate* (a loquacious talker of nonsense). The present writer is fond of simple words like *crumbo, ickle, sneb, pheeze* and perhaps *firk.*

A writer can collaborate with the genius of his native language by exploiting its phonetic peculiarities not to express but to create reality. Mark Twain's short story for children, "A Cat-Tale," revolves around words that contain the sound of *cat:* caterpillar, catechism, catastrophe, Catullus, concatenation, etc. Thoreau used the two meanings of *premises* to indicate the property of the farmer as well as the stipulated conditions on which he based his claims of ownership. In early American literature we find a constant preoccupation with the double meaning of the word "continent" as the continuous land surface of the new American continent unbroken by the sea and also as the Puritan virtue of sexual restraint. Kleist in *The Battle of Arminius* exploits the ambiguity of Ger. *Versprechen* promise/ slip of the tongue; *Ohnmacht* fainting spell/ impotence. Robbe-Grillet's play *La Jalousie* is based on the two meanings of Fr. *jalousie* jealousy/ Venetian blinds, and a short story by Borges on the double meaning of Span. *hoja* sheet of paper/ sword; Marguerite Duras in one of her works plays with the sound of *la menthe anglaise* peppermint/ *l'amante anglaise* the English mistress/ *l'amante en glaise* the clay mistress.

This verbal ambiguity was raised to a creative literary principle by Raymond Roussel, a now forgotten French genius whose plays in the twenties touched off riots in Paris. In his posthumous work, *How I Wrote Certain of My Books,* he explained how he constructed plots based on the multiple meanings of words and phonetic coincidences: *melon* fruit/bowler hat, *louche* ladle/ squint-eyed. By exploiting the sounds and ambiguities of several languages this principle suggests many possibilities: Ger. *Geschichte* history/ fiction, *Anstreicher* house painter/ trickster, *der Fall* the fall of man/ grammatical declension, with overtones of *die Falle* trap or snare, illustrating the close relation between sin and syntax; Rus. *mir* peace/world (Lenin: "We want peace"); Fr. *laide* an ugly woman/ Eng. laid *(la femme la plus laide à Paris)*. Normally, it is the story that produces the words; here the words choose the meaning and create the story. For example, a gory tale could be written around these phonetically related words: organ, organism, orgasm, morgue, Morgan, morganatic, ogre, Hungarian, rogue. Once written down and introduced to one another, these words pursue their course independent of the author, who cannot be held responsible for the ensuing unpleasant complications. This quaint theory of creative composition was given literary prominence by the etymological hypotheses of Gerard Manley Hopkins, who assumed that words similar in sound will also be similar in meaning and probably have a common root.

Unfamiliar or learned words are sometimes modified by the popular ear and assimilated to native sounds, generally in a spirit of playful confusion: pulpit/bullpit, opera/uproar, faux pas/fox pass, Lat. *meretrix* prostitute/merry tricks (Joyce), tureen/Marshal Turenne, who reputedly drank his soup from his helmet, which is very unlikely. A word selects its own associations solely on the basis of phonetic similarity. Much (doubtful) wisdom has been garnered from such coincidences: asses/masses, lock/wedlock, promise/compromise, antics/semantics. In China a clock is never given to one as a gift, for the word *tsung* (clock) happens to be a homonym of "the end of days"; in Japan the number 42 *(shini)* is considered unlucky because it is a homonym of "death." In ancient Rome it was believed that eating hare enhanced one's beauty: *lepus* hare, *lepos* beauty. The cock (Lat. *gallus*), the national symbol of France since the Revolution, owes its popularity in a large measure to the circumstance that it is a homophone of Lat. *gallus* a Gaul; the columbine, Fr. *l'ancolie,* became the symbol of sadness because of its phonetic resemblance to "melancholy." In medical folklore the smell of *new-mown hay* on the breath of a patient is diagnosed as incipient *pneumonia,* and *malaria* as caused by bad air. The apple of Eden was believed to be a peach because of the Fr. *péché* sin. The phonic similarity between Gr. *soma* (body) and *sema* (tomb) suggested the Orphic conception of the body as the grave of the soul, the prison-house where the soul dwells as a stranger until released by death.

The names of saints are often associated in the popular mind with a trade or profession because of some resemblance of sound: St. Vincent is the patron saint of wine growers (Fr. *vin* wine), St. Michel the patron saint of bakers (Fr. *miche* loaf of bread); or a saint's name may be phonetically similar to an ailment that the saint is called upon to cure: those who suffer from eye diseases pray to St. Augustine (Ger. *Auge* eye), the hard of hearing to St. Ouen (Fr. *ouïr* to hear), the lame to St. Lambert (Ger. *lahm* lame), those who limp to St. Cloud (Lat. *claudicantem* limping), those who have the gout to St. Genou (Fr. *genou* knee), and those who suffer from hemorrhoids to St. Audrey, who died of a throat ailment (the connection here being obscure). St. Medard for some reason is depicted in the Middle Ages laughing inanely with his mouth wide open ("le ris de St. Medard"), and is invoked by those who suffer from a toothache.

It is precisely this familiar language that we take for granted, our common mother tongue, that proves to be unreliable. Its very familiarity shields us from large areas of human experience and from the wonders of daily life, "les merveilleux du quotidien." Constant use has dulled our senses so that we comprehend the conventional meaning of opaque words without looking at their configuration or listening to their sound, just as people who live on the seashore do not hear the roar of the waves. What is *bekannt* "familiar" is not *erkannt* "recognized" (Hegel). If the stars came out once a year, Emerson observed, we would all turn out to gaze at them in wonder; or, to quote Heine's example, if a single Jew were left in the world, people would walk miles to shake his hand.

Our thoughts run thoughtlessly along the tracks laid down by the language we happen to speak. In English, for example, certain concepts always go together: (a) in the form of a necessary relationship: *swarthy* refers only to complexion, *shrug* to shoulders, *gnash* to teeth, *capsize* to boats; (b) as ready-made wedded phrases combined for phonetic reasons: bed and board, womb to tomb; (c) accepted modes of thought: *maid* is always qualified by old, *ass* and *goose* (never gander) by silly, *Yankee* by damn (in the South), and *lucre* by filthy, although no derogatory meaning is attached to *lucrative*. One of the ways that critical writers attempt to disrupt these familiar verbal combinations is by dissociation, that is, by making fine distinctions between closely related ideas—e.g., between imitation and emulation, wit and humor, foresight and vision, naked and nude, piety and spirituality. On the tombstone of his dog, Boatswain, who died of madness, Byron placed the following epitaph: "Near this spot are deposited the remains of one who possessed beauty without vanity, strength without insolence, courage without ferocity, and all the virtues of man without his vices." An excellent example of dissociation is Don Juan's description of the Devil's friends in Bernard Shaw's *Man and Superman* (Act III):

. . . They are not beautiful: they are only decorated. They are not clean: they are only shaved and starched. They are not dignified: they are only fashionably dressed. They are not educated: they are only college passmen. They are not religious: they are only pew-renters. They are not moral: they are only conventional. They are not virtuous: they are only cowardly. They are not even vicious: they are only "frail." They are not artistic: they are only lascivious. They are not prosperous: they are only rich. They are not loyal, they are only servile; not dutiful, only sheepish; not public spirited, only patriotic; not courageous, only quarrelsome; not determined, only obstinate; not masterful, only domineering; not self-controlled, only obtuse; not self-respecting, only vain; not kind, only sentimental; not social, only gregarious; not considerate, only polite; not intelligent, only opinionated; not progressive, only factious; not imaginative, only superstitious; not just, only vindictive; not generous, only propitiatory; not disciplined, only cowed. . . .

Dissociation was the subject of a number of interesting studies by Viktor Shklovski, one of the leaders of the Russian formalist movement in the early years of this century, for which he coined the word

"ostranenie" (defamiliarization). In many works devoted to this subject, Shklovski analyzed the different "defamiliarizing" devices employed by Tolstoy, Gogol and Laurence Sterne, among others. A more
extreme form of this concept, known as *za'um,* was set forth by another
writer of the formalist movement, Khlebnikov, who devoted all his
efforts to cleansing and purifying the words of his native language
which had been infected and stained by long years of complicity with
bourgeois culture, having been used as slave labor to support some
external structure such as church, state or political party. Khlebnikov
devised many ways of stripping these words of their traditional associations, principally by breaking up their phonic density or carnal weight
(Leibhaftigkeit, épaisseur), as a plough breaks up the soil. One of the
principal aims of the formalist movement, as announced in its Manifesto, "A Slap in the Face of Public Taste," was to restore the phonemic
appropriateness of Russian words. The sound of the Russian word
maslyanistii (unction) made Andrey Sinayevsky physically ill. Another
writer finds the sound of *zhulik* (thief) and *svinya* (swine) too refined,
and prefers the phonetically more appropriate Hebrew equivalents
ganav and *chazir.* Some of the writers associated with this aggressive
movement went to great lengths to break down familiar words into
new verbal units, even replacing common words with arbitrary phonic
neologisms. "The lily is beautiful," wrote Alexander Kruchenykh, one
of the authors of the Manifesto, "but the word 'lily' *(liliya)* is atrocious;
it has been handled a great deal and raped. I therefore name the lily
'yeouyi' and the old beauty is restored."

VI

Etymology

*"Heaven is where man first crept
upon the floor. . . ."* (Yeats)

*"Wer immer nach Gründen geht, geht
zugrunde. . . ."* (Friedrich Hebbel).

The above quotations reflect diametrically opposed attitudes with respect to etymology as represented by two types of humanity, the genetic and the historical: To the former the basic meaning of things and events is derived from their consecration by our early ancestors in the springtime of the world. All subsequent development has been away from perfection towards degeneration and decay: "All is good as it leaves the hands of the Author of things, all degenerates in the hands of men" (the first sentence of Rousseau's *Emile*). Genetic thinking subordinates all stages of human development to the earliest, which it assumes to be the purest and most significant. We return with reverence to the past for etymological corroboration. This need for continuity finds expression in many genetic metaphors that interpret progress backwards from an advanced to a primitive state of nature, from adulthood to infancy, from the butterfly to the caterpillar, from the luminous fruit to the dark root. Etymology is a genealogical tree of words whose essential nature is revealed in the germinating seed which contains the promise of the future: "As the seed bears in itself the whole nature of the tree and the taste and form of its fruits, so do the first traces of the Spirit virtually contain the whole of History" (Hegel, *Philosophy of History*). A word never frees itself completely from its origin. Despite the modifications and variations it undergoes in the restrictive pattern of the sentence, it still retains the traces of its original identity, like an anonymous recruit on the drill ground who still preserves in the uniform ranks the private broodings and early attachments of his civilian life. "Reality is the naked Alpha not the hierophant Omega. . . . It is an infant A standing on infant legs,/ Not twisted, stooping, polymathic Z" (Wallace Stevens).

Representatives of the historical type, on the other hand, frown on etymological studies. The events of life are irreversible. We must face the terrors of life heroically, confident in the progressive advancement of the human race. The meaning of things must be found not in the dark seed but in the fruit of our labors. A word is an arbitrary conventional sign whose meaning is determined by its function in the sentence, independent of its origin. All efforts to investigate its "birth certificate" and establish its paternity are for the most part misleading and time-consuming. Words do not become old and venerable. They have no memory that reaches across the generations, and no secrets to reveal: "J'ai dit 'pomme' à la pomme, elle m'a dit 'mensonge.' " The genetic habit of mind confuses origin with purpose, and the earliest with the most authentic:

> There is no set of maxims more important for an historian than this: that the actual causes of a thing's origins and its eventual uses, the manner of its incorporation into a system of purposes, are worlds apart: that everything that exists, no matter what its origin, is periodically reinterpreted by those in power in terms of fresh intentions . . . in the course of which

the earlier meaning and purpose are necessarily either obscured or lost. No
matter how well we understand the utility of a certain physiological organ
(or of a legal institution, a custom, a political convention, an artistic genre,
a cultic trait) we do not thereby understand anything of its origin.

(Nietzsche, *The Genealogy of Morals*, Chap. XII)

Romantic theories of language, influenced by the Neapolitan philosopher Vico, hark back to the cradle of human speech when man
thought and spoke in metaphors. He saw his bodily contour in the
world around him: his elbow in Ancona (Gr. *angkón*), his knee in
Genoa (Lat. *genu*), his nose in Lang*eness,* his ear in Helsing*ör,* his eye
in *En* geddi (Heb. *ayin* eye) and his sleeve in *La Manche.* His innocent
imagination pictured Europe as a virgin, with Germany forming the
body, France the bosom, Spain the head, Bohemia the navel, the Alps
the backbone, the branching mountain chains the ribs—a stylistic device known as cosmography that continues to be elaborated: England
is seen as an old shoe, Italy as a boot, India as an udder, the United
States as a wisdom tooth, Mexico as a cornucopia. Primitive man also
conceived analogies in terms of family relations: arrow, the son of the
bow; echo, daughter of the voice; lion, the father of roaring. These
genealogical metaphors are common in Arabic and known as *kunya,*
but are also found in Western languages: soot, brother of flickering fire
(Aeschylus); coughing, stepmother of the chest (Matthew of Ven-
dôme); urine, the soft-flowing daughter of Fright (Coleridge). The act
of memory for modern man, according to Vico, involves the effort to
regain these half-forgotten images and to reconstruct the metaphorical
process whereby primitive man gave shape to his perception of the
world around him.

Our conception of the origin of things determines to a great extent
our basic philosophy and overall attitudes. According to Freud, for
example, human civilization began when man first repressed his infantile urge to put out blazes by playful urination contests and directed
it to higher social ends, such as roasting animals and forging weapons.
Women, being retromingent, were entrusted to tend the domestic fires
as guardians of the hearth, thus permitting the men to devote them-

selves to hunting, fishing and the defense of the tribe. This theory that makes civilized life dependent on the continuous and permanent repression of the instincts, with the inevitable symptoms of neurosis and madness, is repugnant to all progressive thinkers, especially Marxists. Human civilization began not with the repression of the urge to put out fires but with the stealing of fire from the gods for the benefit of man by Prometheus, regarded by Marx as "the foremost saint and martyr in the philosophical calendar," the forerunner of the proletarian revolution ordained by historical destiny. The voice that proclaimed this bright future for mankind was the voice of Pro-metheus (literally, forthought), but the hands were those of his younger brother Epimetheus (afterthought), who opened Pandora's box of plagues, which almost destroyed mankind.

The past history of a word does not determine its present use and is of little interest except as it is taken to illustrate some general principle or as a display of anecdotal erudition:

DIXIE, from Fr. *dix* ten, which appeared on the reverse side of the ten-dollar note issued in Louisiana before the Civil War.

FORNICATE, Lat. *fornix* arch or vault (of an underground Roman brothel), came to denote the pudendous activity beneath it.

VAUDEVILLE, from Vau de Vire in Normandy, where songs were highly prized in the fifteenth century.

CROISSANT, the name of a French milk-roll, so called because of its crescent shape, is a translation of Ger. *Hörnchen* little horn, the first rolls of this shape having been made in Vienna in the seventeenth century to commemorate the decisive victory over the Turks, whose national emblem is the Crescent.

It is of doubtful value, for example, for a cook to know that OMELET comes from Fr. *omelette*, by metathesis *alemette:* Lat. *lametta* small plate; that RHUBARB was imported from the Volga

River in Russia (Gr. *rha* the Volga + *barbaron* foreign); that *SATIRE* originally referred to a composite dish of assorted fruit and vegetables (Lat. *satura*), hence a mixed literary composition; and that *MAYONNAISE*, earlier *MAHONNAISE*, comes from Port Mahón, the capital of Minorca, whence it spread all over the world.

Words stray from home and their origins are soon forgotten. Many familiar things have traveled far from the place of their birth, leaving little trace of their origin: *Arcadia* left its mountainous home in ancient Greece and became an ideal state of rural felicity; *Utopia*, which is no place at all (Gr. *ou* no + *topos* place) has become a commonplace; *bayonet* came from Bayonne in France; *cantaloupe*, from Cantalupe in Italy; *cravat*, from Croatia; *pistol*, from Pistoia in Italy; and *spaniel*, from Spain.

We no longer see ale in brid*al*, ass in *eas*el, boor in neigh*bor*, heel in in*culc*ate, horse in wal*rus*, rope in stir*rup*, smoke in per*fume*, straw in *stipul*ation, udder in ex*uber*ance. We do not hear the howl in *owl*, the drumbeats in *pariah*, the whistle in per*sif*lage, the whisper in *ink*ling, the tuning of a musical instrument in *incen*tive, or the sound of convivial drinking in *lampoon*, *hobnob* and sym*pos*ium. Even the educated native is unlikely to be aware of the close etymological relation between ink and caustic, cosmetics and cosmos, infant and infantry, muscle and mouse, lewd and laity, sad and sated, vinegar and eager, vanilla and vagina, whore and charity. Conversely, we sometimes see what is not there: *anal* in analysis, *arse* in arsenal, *male* in malevolent, *the rapist* in therapist, *laughter* in manslaughter.

Scatymology or Repressed Origins

The highest flights of human thought take their wings from lowly matter. "It is from the flames of passion that philosophy lights its torch" (Marquis de Sade). Our noblest words are rooted in sense impressions: inspiration in breath, spirit in wind, tact in touch, obedience in hearing, sagacity in the sense of smell. The metaphysical is at first physical. All our knowledge is basically carnal and is rooted in the body, which is the source of all things: "All is seared with toil,/ And wears man's image and shares man's smell" (G.M. Hopkins). Yet we are nettled by the soiled roots of words, for they remind us of our animal origins and distract us from our quest for moral perfection. We would prefer a prophylactic language defecated of all sensible matter, a "Language that goes easy as a glove/ O're good and evil, smoothens both to one" (Robert Browning).

Thus, we would rather not see stable in *constable* (count + stable), filth in *gory* (OE *gor* dirt, mud), excrement in *poppycock* (Dut. *pappekak* soft dung), posteriors in *recoil* (Lat. *re* back + *culus* buttocks), testicles in *orchids* (Gr. *orchis* testicle), or the male genitals in *fascination* (Lat. *fascinum* membrum virile, an image of which was hung around the necks of children as a charm against witchcraft). We ignore the rubbing sound of copulation in *fidget* (ME *föken,* vulgar; Ger. *ficken*); we close our ears to the sound of flatulence in *decrepit* and and *discrepancy* (Lat. *crepitare* to make a sharp, crackling noise), in *feisty* (ME *fist* emission of gastronomic gas), in *pumpernickel* (Ger. *pumpern* to break wind + *Nickel* dimin. of Nicholas), and perhaps in *partridge* (written by Joyce *phartridge,* to indicate the flatulent noise made by its wings on rising); *skulduggery* is an American variation of Scottish *skulduddery,* illicit sexual intercourse, a euphemistic alteration of *adultery*.

Guesstymologies

There are many words in our language, more than we generally suppose, whose origin is completely unknown, even common words such as: awning, basket, burglar, bias, capsize, clever, dodge, fluke, fun, garbage, golf, job, lad, oar, put, riot, shark, tantrum, wallet. We do not find this lack of information disturbing. We consult the dictionary for the correct spelling or acceptable pronunciation of a word and seldom for its etymology.

Many more words are of uncertain, dubious or obscure origin and are indicated as such in our dictionaries, often followed by probable or assumed etymologies, by plausible but unscientific conjectures. Is *bungle* derived from Swed. *bangla* to work ineffectively, Gypsy *bongo* awkward, or an echoic combination of *bongle* + *bumble?* Is a *bonfire* a *bon(e) fire* in which corpses, often of saints, were burned; or is it a fire kindled on the receipt of good news (Fr. *bon* good)? Does *condom* come from the name of its eighteenth-century inventor or from Lat. *condoma* cover, dome, roof? Does *hunch,* intuitive guess, come from a gambler's belief that it brings luck to touch the hump of a *hunch* back? Does *cocksure* refer to the fowl *cock* or to *cock* in the sense of "tap"; or is it a corrupt form of *godsure?*

BIGOT is sometimes taken to be a corrupt form of Visigoth or of the St. Augustine order of the *Beguttae;* it has also been derived from Span. *hombre de bigotes,* referring to a man of the Flemish retinue of Charles V, hence a man of resolute mien who swore tremendous oaths through his heavy mustache, such as: *bei Gott;* perhaps from Fr. *bigote,* a small roll with sugar for children in the form of a mustache; it is usually derived from the reply of Rollo, the duke of the Normans, to Charles the Simple, king of the West Franks, when he refused to kiss the latter's foot, saying: *Nese, bi got!* (No, by God!).

HOCUS-POCUS, (a) from a mock expression invented by jugglers and conjurers; (b) a corruption of Lat. *hoc est corpus* from the words of the Eucharist, alluding to transubstantiation; (c) from "Ochus Bochus," the supposed demon of Scandinavian mythology; (d) from Lat. *iocus* a joke, originally a verbal game, with diminutive form *ioculus;* and (e) in popular etymology from Ital. *O, che poco,* erroneously translated "O, how cheap," instead of "O, how little."

HUMBUG, Irish *uim-bog* soft copper or false coin; or Ital. *uomo bugiardo* a lying man; also from the name of the city Hamburg, the center from which false coins came to England during the Napoleonic Wars; also taken to be a corruption of *hum and haw,* to temporize.

STERLING, from the name of "Easterlings" given to the North German merchants who came to England in the reign of Edward I. However, the word is found before the time of Edward I, and it has been suggested that it comes from OE *steorling* little star, stamped on an early coin, such as may be found on some of William II; another conjecture derives the word from OE *staerling* starling, which may have been the dove on the coins of Edward the Confessor.

WHIG, a short form of *whiggamer* (*whig,* an echoic Scottish word for urging on horses + *mare* horse; or from the initials of the motto of the Scots Covenanters: *W*e *h*ope *i*n *G*od; the name *whig* has also been associated with *whey* sour milk, an unkind reference to the sour-milk faces of the western Lowlanders.

Poetymology, or the Poet's Pursuit of Etymological Rejuvenation

The poet seeks to recall the forgotten Latin and Greek roots of English words to the (learned) reader and thus restore their original unfamiliar sense: e.g., *perplexed* (twisted) walks, *sincere* (unadulterated) wine, *latent* (concealed) nets, *generous* (not degenerate) horses. Paul Valéry speaks of *scrupulous* brooks (Lat. *scrupulus* a small sharp stone), Milton of *secure* delight (Lat. *se* + *cura* free from care) and *affable* archangel (Lat. *affabilis* easy to talk to), Charles Doughty of *austere* fruit (Gr. *hauos* dry) and *eager* wine (OE *aigre* sour, keen), Thomas Hardy of *vespering* birds, birds that fly west in the early evening (*vesper,* cognate with Gr. *hesperus,* refers to both *west* and *evening,* as does Ger. *Abend*). In the line "The full-juiced apple, waxing over-mellow," Tennyson recalls the original meaning of *wax* to grow (Ger. *wachsen*), now archaic except with reference to the moon; and in the line "The erudite moon is up," Ezra Pound revives the root meaning of *erudite* (Lat. *ex* + *rudis* cleared of roughness, purified).

A more violent method of etymological rejuvenation is to inject a hyphen into the bosom of a word in order to extract some hidden meaning or superimposed intention. The poet Valéry thus speaks of his "cor-respondence" to indicate that his letters come from his heart (Lat. *cor* heart); and Claudel, of "con-naissance" to indicate that consciousness is equivalent to rebirth and that man's memory reaches back beyond his brief existence. Antonin Artaud hyphenates "po-ema" (Gr. *po* + *ema* blood) so as to evoke the *hem*orrhagic reality of poetic creation. Paul Celan places a hyphen in the German word *Men-schen* (human beings) in order to reveal the essential unity of mankind (Eng. men + Chin. *shen* people). Some of the early German rationalists put a hyphen in words like "Ro-man" and "Ger-man" to emphasize the universal nature of man's national allegiance. The master of this device, however, was the existential German philosopher Martin Heidegger, who employed it as a habitual technique to extract hidden roots and primal origins. A typical Heideggerian example is the word *Schlag-wort* (slogan) which stresses the striking and beating *(schlagen)* at the root of the word. The English poet Gerard Manley Hopkins often employed the rhetorical device of tmesis to separate parts of an indivisible word by inserting an intervening word or words instead of a hyphen; e.g., "Brim, in a flash, full," thus restoring the original force of the dead suffix in "brimful."

Letters have at different times been inserted in words by scholars to make them conform to a supposed Latin or Greek derivation; and these, unlike the attempts of the poets, have found their way into the dictionary and have become part of the language. Thus, the letter *b* was erroneously inserted in humble, slumber, thimble; *c* in scythe, scent; *d* in admiral, thunder, scoundrel; *h* in catholic, author, posthumous, theater; *l* in calm, could, almond; *n* in passenger; *s* in spruce, scissors; *t* in peasant; *w* in whore. For such misguided pseudo-corrections the Germans have coined the blend word *verschlimmbessern,* to impair or disfigure an object while attempting to improve it. The *i* in the earlier correct spelling of "women" (wimen) and the *u* in "wonder" (wunder) were changed to an *o* for cosmetic reasons since the original forms written in longhand appeared illegible: *ꞁꞷꞃꞷ* ; *ꞃꞷꞃꞣꞷ* wimen; wunder. Some radical feminists have adopted the original spelling which effaces the incriminating suffix *-man*. Similarly, for greater orthographic clarity, the original spelling of *irritibility* was changed to the current *irritability*.

Context Is All

A word in the dictionary leads an absurd existence. It reminds us of the ancient Greek who carried in his bag a single brick as a sample of the house he wished to sell. Meaning is not inherent in solitary words but in their relations to one another. Once a word is admitted into the fraternity of the sentence, it abandons its former associations and accommodates itself to the arbitrary conventions of a new order of discourse. To look for "louse" in the dictionary between "lounge" and "lout"—instead of between the thumb and the forefinger—is an odd habit of foreigners and pedants, erudition on the wrong scent. The meaning of a word depends on the context in which it is found:

> In an ant's house a drop of dew is a flood (Eastern proverb). On a man's nose an inch is a long distance (Irish proverb). How small Mt. Horeb looks when Moses is standing on it (Heine). Footnotes in Japanese books are found on top of the page. In China the seat of honor is on the left, so that the psalmist's "sit on my right hand" is rendered in the Chinese version "sit on my left hand."

> A librarian who does not read beyond the title page of a book, for whom the Italians have coined the word *frontispizzaio,* can easily be misled in cataloguing new books. Thus, a book on *Irish Bulls* was catalogued under zoology, Hemingway's *Across the River and into the Trees* under golf, Chapman's *Homer* under baseball, Martin Buber's *Between Man and Man* under pornography, Virginia Woolf's biography of Elizabeth Barrett Browning's cocker spaniel, *Flush,* under toilets.

> In the Romance languages an adjective has a different meaning, depending on whether it precedes or follows the noun: Span. *pobre hombre* poor man (without money), *hombre pobre* poor man (to be

pitied); Fr. *musique sacrée* sacred music, *sacrée musique* damn music. In English a chestnut horse is not a horse chestnut, a Venetian blind not a blind Venetian, a day off not an off day, a woman model not a model woman.

Our comprehension of things depends on the nature of our past experience, our prejudices, conscious and unconscious, our angle of vision and shifting perspectives which differ from individual to individual. How the same event can be differently interpreted by different viewers has been admirably illustrated in two famous works: Edith Wharton's novel *Ethan Frome* and in Robert Browning's long poem *The Ring and the Book*. People are differently affected by the same object: *duo si faciunt idem, non est idem* the same thing said or done by two people is not the same:

A fool does not see the same tree that a wise man sees (Blake); the "speculation" of a thinker is not that of a banker; a tailor, a suitor and a plaintiff "press their suits" in different ways; both a writer and a madman may be "committed"; a barrister as well as a drunkard may be found "moaning at the bar," as also Tennyson's sailor poet who hopes to see his Pilot face to face.

What's sauce for the goose is not necessarily sauce for the gander; a *fallen* man is a hero, a *fallen* woman has departed from rectitude. What is permitted to Jove is not permitted to the ox: *quod licit Jovi non licit bovi*. What is desirable in an animal may be undesirable in man and vice versa. In animals God declared unfit the broken and the maimed (Lev. 22:22), but in man he declared desirable the broken and contrite heart (Ps. 51:17). In Christian iconography the fatal apple held by Eve is the symbol of man's downfall, but when held by the Virgin Mary the symbol of man's salvation.

Ibsen once remarked that whereas *he* went down into the sewer to clean it, Zola went there to take a bath.

There are many ways of looking at things (cf. Carl Sandburg, *Elephants Are Different to Different People,* and Wallace Stevens, *Thirteen Ways of Looking at a Blackbird*). The various ways of viewing elephants and blackbirds in these two poems do not represent different aspects of reality. Although partial and incomplete, these views are open to inspection and public discussion. The viewers do not live in different worlds cut off from one another. Mutual understanding is possible and the notion of objective truth need not be abandoned. This can be illustrated in an example given by Chesterton:

> Four men meet under the same lamp post; one to paint it pea green as part of a great municipal reform; one to read his breviary in the light of it; one to embrace it with accidental ardor in a fit of alcoholic enthusiasm; and the last merely because the pea green post is a conspicuous point of rendezvous with his young lady.
>
> (Quoted by Charles Frankel, *The Case for Modern Man,* Beacon Press, 1956, p. 80)

In our Western theory of government we assume that the four men can live in peace and harmony without clearly defined mutual goals, that they are reasonable enough to recognize their personal interest in keeping the post well lit and in good repair and, guided by their natural reciprocal sympathies, not to infringe on the rights of others. Numerous unforeseen incidents will no doubt occur that might require adjudication and perhaps police intervention. The individuals involved, however, need not surrender their rights to an all-powerful state with the power to decide the disputed points on the basis of an explicit ideology that is not subject to argument or compromise, to civil morality or world opinion.

This sanguine view of human nature with its attendant notions of tolerance and good fellowship in a pluralistic society has a special attraction for Americans. It finds its classical expression in the speech given by Benjamin Franklin at the conclusion of the deliberations at the Constitutional Convention of 1787 in which he urged his fellow-members to set aside their differences and ratify the proposed constitution despite its imperfections, to suppress their private convictions, however impassioned, and to be guided by a spirit of accommodation, working compromises, mutual concessions and partial agreements. What we now take to be an imperfection may in time turn out to be a blessing through the workings of the Invisible Hand. We need not know the ultimate Truth to live and prosper (cf. opposed and conflicting proverbs: Faint heart never won fair lady/ Look before you leap). If we strive for perfection and absolute Truth, we may never have a constitution. This compromise with truth and personal conviction astonished German thinkers who scorned a political theory that recognized practical motives of expediency to the detriment of unsullied Truth.[1] This binocular way of looking at things (i.e., to see a bat as a bird *and* a mouse at the same time) is known as Janusian thinking, after Janus, the god who faced two ways, protector of doors and entrances, from whom we also derive the lowly *janitor.*

---

[1]Germany's defeat in the last war led to a reappraisal of its political tradition and to a greater appreciation of the American view. In his comprehensive work on truth, *Von der Wahrheit* (untranslated), published soon after the end of the war, Karl Jaspers devoted the final chapter to a favorable review of the "Franklinsche Prinzip."

VII

Eye and Ear in the Creation of Language

OF THE FIVE BODILY SENSES THROUGH WHICH WE INTERPRET THE WORLD around us, three are of little use in the formation of permanent ideas. The sense of touch, the lowest and most indecent of all the senses, is associated with tactless gropings and incriminating fingerprints and with the nimble fingers of magicians, pickpockets, card sharks and chiropractors. The sense of touch was described by Aristotle as a disgrace, an opinion often quoted to justify ascetic practices, especially sexual continence. It is the sense we ultimately rely upon when we doubt the testimony of the other senses, as did the doubting apostle Thomas who would not believe unless he saw and *touched* Jesus (John 20:25). Taste, which is the sense of touch restricted to the tongue (OE *tasten* to touch), is a highly subjective sense doubly locked behind teeth and lips and one that makes for interminable disputes. The sense of smell is related to intuitive wisdom: *sagacity*, Latin *sagax* keen scent; Rus. *chutkost* olfactory sensitivity; Heb. *re'ah* smell is related in the

Talmud to *ru'ah* spirit.[1] The sense of smell is the least intellectual of
the senses. Odors arouse the emotions without engaging the mind, so
that we can speak of a man of taste or vision but not of smells. For
purposes of social communication, odors are too elusive to be sustained
with precision or consistency, too vehement and hypnotic to be reproduced or properly directed. The two remaining senses seem to be the
most reliable in guiding us through the stubborn world of matter: the
eye through which man enters the world, and the ear through which
the world enters man.

No one mode of perception can be said to be the exclusive agent
of knowledge. When one sense seeks dominance it impoverishes itself
and, even when illumined by the intellect or stirred by the imagination,
becomes feeble and obscure:

> The Eye of Man a little narrow orb, clos'd up & dark,
> Scarcely beholding the great light, conversing with the Void;
> The Ear a little shell, in small volutions shutting out
> All melodies & comprehending only Discord and Harmony;
> The Tongue a little moisture fills, a little food it cloys,
> A little sound it utters & its cries are faintly heard,
> Then brings forth Moral Virtue the cruel Virgin Babylon.
>   Can such an Eye judge of the stars? & looking thro' its tubes
> Measure the sunny rays that point their spears on Udanadan?
> Can such an Ear, fill'd with the vapours of the yawning pit,
> Judge of the pure melodious harp struck by a hand divine?
> Can such closed Nostrils feel a joy? or tell of autumn fruits

---

[1]In commenting on this etymological relationship the Talmud informs us that the true
Messiah will be recognized by a highly developed olfactory sense that will enable him
to ferret out heretics and detect saints. A long nose in Hebrew is synonymous with
patience and long-suffering, denoting in its owner intense religious fervor if not strong
powers of cogitation. A more skeptical view holds that a long nose, although proper
for elephants who depend on this organ, must in man be condemned as unesthetic. The
entire subject of noses, however, is surrounded by extravagant views and an inordinate
amount of vanity.

When grapes & figs burst their covering to the joyful air?
Can such a Tongue boast of the living waters?. . .
                              —William Blake, *Milton*, I.5

At the end of the last century Ernst Heinrich Haeckel, the renowned German zoologist, set forth the theory that man began his evolutionary career as a deaf mute and hence was obliged to employ written signs in order to communicate. This view of the origin of language in which the eye is dominant finds support in a Chinese legend according to which the earliest communication was brought to man in the form of signs inscribed on a turtle's back. Not the sounds that came from that reptile's toothless beak but the markings on its carapace were to serve man as a model in decoding nature's secrets!

The dominance of the ear in the creation of language was formulated at the end of the eighteenth century by the German philosopher and poet Johann Gottfried von Herder as follows: "When man first saw the lamb, he noticed that it was white, wooly and gentle; but it was only when it began to bleat that man perceived its real essence, and burst forth: 'Ah, you are the bleating one!' " This theory came to be known as "the myth of the bleating lamb." The visual and tactile characteristics of the lamb could be distinguished and remembered only when associated with sound, which then became an integral part of the word's meaning (Fr. *bêler* to bleat > *bélier* ram). The name given to the elephant was not based on the shape of its lithe proboscis or the texture of its wrinkled skin but on the sound of its roaring. The bat, to take a more modest example, received its name not from its blindness (Span. *murciélago*), baldness (Fr. *chauve-souris*), shyness (Ital. *pipistrello*), leathery skin (Swed. *Läderlapp*), its preference for the night (Gr. *nukteris*) or resemblance to a mouse (Ger. *Fledermaus*), but from its most prominent characteristic: the sound of its flapping wings (Arab. *watwat*).

Animal noises, however, do not become words. We do not call a sheep a *baa-baa* or a dog a *bow-wow*—rare exceptions being the Chinese word for cat *miuh* and the Greenlandic word for goat *mek-mek*. Human speech arose only after the instinctive cries of the forest were aban-

doned. Man perceived and organized the world not through the senses
he has in common with the animals but on principles inherent in the
mind. The rendering of animal sounds is a culturally determined recon-
struction differently conceived in the various languages. The bark of
a dog is heard in English as *bow-wow,* in French as *gnaf-gnaf,* in Spanish
as *guau,* in Hebrew as *hav-hav,* in Japanese as *wanwan.* The *moo* of the
cow cannot be its real sound because, as is well known, the cow cannot
round her lips to produce an initial labial, no matter how successful it
may be with the following vowel.

The cockcrow heard by the English ear, *cockadoodledoo* (in Shakespeare's day *cock-a-diddle-dow*), the Fr. *coquerico,* Rum. *cucurigu,* Ital.
chicchirichi or Dan. *kykeliky* are all fanciful reconstructions which
Chanticleer himself would regard with amused contempt. Of all the
versions of that alarming matutinal noise, none is more fantastic than
the Manchu *dchor dchor,* unless it were the bassoon-like Algonquin
cockcrow *pahpahahquau* (I quote from memory), for both versions lack
the cock's characteristic *k-*sound and are hence not in keeping with the
nature of that ill-humored fowl. The jubilant crow of the herald of the
dawn as reproduced by the oboe in the second part of Haydn's *The
Seasons* is generally acknowledged by students of animal phonetics as
more worthy of the King of the Barnyard. The present writer cannot
pronounce judgment on the finer shades of the cock's musical performance since, as a city dweller, he has never been trained to identify
barnyard sounds with confidence, however insistent, or assess their
precise effects—a bear, as the Russians say, having stepped into his ear.
There is no need, however, to examine the various theories concerning
the nature of the cockcrow with respect to tone, timbre and phonetic
pattern, for these are incapable of variation or improvement and hence
not subject to approval or disapproval. Having heard one cockcrow,
you've heard them all. The cock cannot dissemble its spasmodic inflections and learn to bray, cackle or hum. Nor can it choose to be silent.
It must crow when in a crowing mood. Crowing belongs to the species
and cannot be detached from its physical context. A cock by definition
is an animal that crows. However remarkable its vocal efforts, it is
nevertheless debarred from human articulation not because it is

phonetically defective but because it is semantically blocked.

Historians have estimated that it was not until about the year 3500 B.C. that man first committed the invisible spoken word to a white surface by means of graphic signs. This ancillary means for recording the human voice marked a turning point in the history of civilization for it created in man a new state of awareness and a clarity of perception unknown to oral communication. It made the sense of vision the dominant metaphor of knowing and put, so to speak, the *voir* in *savoir*. In time, writing became the prerogative of an elite class of priests, scholars and clerks and was regarded as a kind of magic. The word "glamour," earlier *glammer,* is a dissimilated variation of "grammar," in the sense of occult learning or secret knowledge. The acquisition of this power introduced an additional spirit of enmity between castle and cathedral, that is, between men of action (nobles, warriors, kings) and men of contemplation (scholars, priests, poets), between those who make history and those who immortalize their achievements in the poems we sing.

The introduction of writing did not supplant the living voice. Men were loathe to entrust the perpetuation of their thoughts and traditions to the impersonal artifice of the written word. Reading continued to be accompanied by vocal mnemonic aids, typographical devices of cantillation and punctuation marks to permit the voice to be heard through the mute signs of the text. Silent reading was unheard of. For many centuries "to read" meant "to read aloud" (Ger. *lesen* = *vorlesen*). In his *Confessions* (VI.3) St. Augustine recounts how during his visit to Milan in A.D. 384 he noted as a matter of surprise that Bishop Ambrose was reading in silence without moving his lips, perhaps the first man to do so. Simple folk were constantly amazed at the magical power of written characters that speak to us from out of the pages of a book. One such early account is recorded in the tenth chapter of Grimmelhausen's *The Adventurous Simplicissimus,* the well-known German picaresque novel of the Thirty Years' War written in 1669:

> Now when first I saw the hermit read the Bible, I could not conceive with whom he should speak so secretly and, as I thought, so earnestly; for well I saw the moving of his lips, yet no man that spake with him........

Yet I answered him: "If I be a man as thou art, so must I likewise be able to see in these black lines what thou canst see: how then may I understand thy words? Dear father, teach me in truth how to understand this matter."

So said he: " 'Tis well, my son, and I will teach thee so that thou mayest speak with these figures as well as I: only 'twill need time, in which I must have patience and thou industry."

The eye has often been described as the most masculine of the sense organs, that is, the most discriminating and the least biased. It can focus without on any object it chooses to contemplate. We need but open our eyes and the world is revealed to us at a glance. Its cognitive and moral claims, however, have been highly exaggerated. It is a credulous organ, greedy for novel sensations and, if not kept in leash by the intellect, easily hoodwinked: "We are led to believe a lie/ When we see with and not through the eye" (Blake). The age-old complaint of moralists has always been directed against the eye as a fertile source of error, deception and untold suffering: "How wise Nature did decree/ With the same eyes to weep and see" (Andrew Marvell).[2]

Attempts to refine the eye's untrustworthy mode of perception by means of artificial contrivances, such as magnifying glasses, microscopes and mirrors, have only succeeded in revealing a strangely hostile, spectral world.[3] Had the eye been meant to look at things closely, like

---

[2]The dominating power of the eye was the basic principle of the Panopticon, the name that Bentham gave to his proposed circular prison with cells fully exposed toward a central well from which an all-seeing optical mechanism could observe the inmates at all times. Similar surveillance mechanisms were later adopted where large areas had to be inspected and controlled, such as army camps, hospitals, workhouses, often provided with peepholes, blinds and open-door lavatories. This disclosed a satanic view of a future society where all men will be fully controlled and will find freedom intolerable, thus fulfilling Lenin's dream of a perfect state.

[3]This may explain Goethe's ill-concealed aversion for bespectacled visitors in whose presence he felt ill at ease and at a tactical disadvantage. He suspected their hostile designs to penetrate his inner life and catch him unawares. Among social creatures a direct stare is unnerving and is resented. Is this because predators stare fixedly at prospective prey before attacking them?

"an old tailor peering at the eye of a needle" (a Dantean image), we would have been provided with a different pair of eyes: "Why has not man a microscopic eye?/ For this plain reason, man is not a fly" (Blake). To Swift's naked eye, Celia looked like a goddess. The gloomy Dean should have been content with this pleasing deception and not have looked at her image in the glass which disclosed her crystal eye, false hair, rough skin and flabby dugs. Such an exact revelation of human growth and decay diminishes human sympathy and dispels all notions of chivalry. The world is best viewed at a distance with half-closed eyes, as an artist views his painting. Things lose their identity when seen on a scale that is not appropriate to them. The human eye was not meant to pierce the veil that hides from us nature's secrets: "If we had a keen vision and feeling of all ordinary human life, it would be like hearing the grass grow and the squirrel's heart beat, and we should die of that roar which lies on the other side of silence" (George Eliot, *Middlemarch,* II.20).[4]

The relative merits of the eye and ear, or of the written and spoken word, have been the subject of constant dissension in all important spheres of thought: in philosophy, religion, pedagogy and literature. The first man in the Western world to perceive the harmful effects of writing was Plato (end of *Phaedrus*). Written words are anonymous: they do not know to whom they are speaking nor, when questioned, how to defend themselves. They merely serve to recall what we already know. Reliance on written documents weakens the memory, provides loopholes to deceive the unwary, creates in the learned a false sense of security based on secondary knowledge and, being accessible to immature minds, opens the door to all kinds of mischievous interpretations. These objections to the written word are repeated by Plato in his *Seventh Letter,* which concludes with the observation: "Every serious man in dealing with really serious subjects avoids writing."

---

[4]In Isaac Babel's fine short story, *Line and Color,* Kerensky refused to wear glasses that would correct his myopic vision, fearing that glasses would reveal too much of the world's naked truth and deprive him of many comforting illusions.

To Aristotle, on the other hand, the eye was "the first gate of the senses," the organ that provides us with mental images indispensable to the development of memory and thought. Writing detaches a word from the immediate life of the speaker and makes it available for scrutiny and reflection. It may be objected that the written word cannot render the visible gestures that supplement our inarticulate aposiopeses. In writing, for example, we cannot snap our fingers, hold our nose, smirk, ogle or wink. This seeming deficiency, however, only demonstrates the superiority of writing over speaking in that it prevents nature from intruding into the cultural world of written forms. It is precisely the dead words of the written text that can be studied and repeated and made to serve the growing needs of civilized life. The scribes who were dedicated to the preservation of the written texts became in time the dominant literary class. The victory of this class is celebrated in Jacques-Louis David's famous painting, *The Death of Socrates,* which depicts the final defeat of this pre-literate hero as he is about to drink the hemlock surrounded by his disciples, among them Plato, who is seated at the foot of the bed absorbed in deep contemplation.

The controversy between eye and ear runs throughout the history of religious thought. Rational theologians measure progress in religion by the advance of visual representations over the seductive power of tribal incantation, when ears are converted to eyes: "All the people *saw* the thunderings . . . and the noise of the trumpets" (Exod. 20:18). God's voice is seen and confirmed in His works. Seeing is believing. To the more pious, however, the supreme religious organ is the ear, for faith cometh from hearing: *ex auditu fides.* To hear is the same as to obey (Lat. *ob* toward + *audire* to hear). "Blessed are those who have *not* seen and yet believe" (John 20:29). Blind Isaac was deceived when he smelled and touched Jacob, but he recognized his voice: the voice was the voice of Jacob and the hands were the hands of Esau.

Judaism attaches the greatest importance to the ear as the most reliable bodily organ. From the earliest times it resisted the seductive eye that leads to the worship of graven images and hence spiritualized all expressions of God's corporeality: "Ye saw no form but only a voice" (Deut. 4:12). In his biblical commentary Spinoza states that the words of the Decalogue were not heard above the din of lightning and thunder at the foot of Mount Sinai (according to Maimonides only the words of the first two commandments were heard distinctly). This enlightened view of revelation teaches us that the Voice from Sinai receives its articulation in a continuous exegetical interpretation of the oral law that stretches from the dim past to a distant future, a never-ending human activity which, properly speaking, constitutes "the education of the human race" (Lessing).

In the field of pedagogy the controversy between eye and ear revolves around the early years of a child's education when oral speech gives way to reading and writing, which soon become the dominant mode of communication. The auditory image now grows fainter and fainter and by the time of adolescence is practically lost, so that the learning of foreign languages becomes increasingly difficult. The child's eyes are taught to scan the printed page for meaning alone and soon acquire the habit of staring and need to be strengthened by corrective glasses.[5] By this time the child's imaginative and creative growth is seriously impaired. Rousseau was aware of this unfortunate development in the early education of children and in his famous work on education was moved to write: "Reading is the curse of childhood. . . . the child who reads ceases to think" *(A Savoyard Priest).*

In learning to read, the child's tender mind is at the same time being indoctrinated with the socially approved myths of patriotism, economic well-being, etc. Great educators such as Pestalozzi and Rudolf Steiner therefore discouraged early reading and stressed independent

---

[5]Proof reading strengthens the tired eye muscles by compelling the eye to trace the contours of the individual letters and deliberately ignore the meaning of the words, a procedure that is opposite to that followed in reading. Proof reading exercises the muscles of the eye at the cost of dulling the mind and robbing it of its freedom. The unhappy fate of the menial copyist who spent his life tracing lifeless letters of the alphabet was a common literary theme around the middle of the last century, for example: Akaky Akakyevich, the hero of Gogol's masterpiece, *The Overcoat;* Nemo, the drug-destroyed copyist in Dickens' *Bleak House;* Melville's *Bartleby, the Scrivener;* and Conan Doyle's Jabez Wilson in *The Red-Headed League* who eked out a living by slavishly copying articles from the *Encyclopedia Britannica.*

observation as the foundation of all knowledge. Many conservative thinkers, on the other hand, favored the rise of reading and literary education among the lower classes since it helped to dissipate the boredom and resentment that came with urban industrialization, made them forget their claim to a just share of the national wealth and, by spreading common notions in novels and romances among all the classes, reinforced existing social unity.

Compulsory universal education then completes the injurious process by making the reader a victim of propaganda and advertising and encouraging him to speak of things he does not understand, a form of enslavement found only in advanced and not in pre-literate cultures:

> . . . the primary function of writing as a means of communication is to facilitate the enslavement of other human beings. The use of writing for disinterested ends, and with a view to the satisfaction of the mind in the fields of science or the arts, is a secondary result of its invention—and may be no more than a way of reinforcing, justifying, or dissimulating its primary function.
>
> (Claude Levi-Strauss, "A Writing Lesson," *A World on the Wane,* New York, 1961, p. 292)

Behind the antagonism of eye and ear looms the larger question concerning the contemplative versus the active life. The ear inclines one to obedience, involvement, engagement and responsibility but also to compulsion, submission and enslavement (Ger. *hörig* from *hören* to hear, has these meanings). The eye, on the other hand, creates distance, the condition for aloofness, detachment and quiet analysis. The joys of contemplation are the perennial theme of philosophers and poets. Lucretius in his immortal poem (beginning of Bk. II) tells of how sweet it is to watch a shipwreck form from a sheltered retreat on the shore and to see men contending and struggling with the elements, not to gloat over their misfortune but to be grateful for our own good fortune—a thought summed up more bluntly by Mark Twain: "We like to see people in trouble, if it doesn't cost us anything" (*Following the Equator,* xlviii).

VIII

Man's Envy of the Dumb Animals

THE HOSTILITY THAT AROSE BETWEEN MAN AND THE ANIMALS IS ONE OF
the saddest chapters in our history. The sudden appearance (intrusion)
of man abrogated the pact between Nature and her creatures. A struggle
now began for the conquest of the planet, a struggle waged over
countless years until the animal world was finally subjugated. Man and
beast inhabit two kingdoms ruled by conflicting interests and governed
by incompatible impulses. They have nothing to say to each other. Man
looks upon the animals as game to be hunted, roasted (sometimes alive)
and eaten. No wonder that they instinctively avoid him and consider
it a misfortune to be in his vicinity. In Hogarth's cruelty series (1751)
we see boys torturing cats and dogs and a coachman beating a starved
nag. Animals are defenseless against man, and it was not until 1822 that
Parliament passed the first laws in their favor. They could only dream
of revenge in a "topsy-turvy world" in which conventional roles are
reversed, a common theme in the sixteenth century illustrated in many

woodcuts of that day in which the ox becomes the butcher, sheep shear shepherds, hares catch and roast hunters, an ass plays the lute.

Man adds insult to injury by attributing human vices to animals, generally based on erroneous conceptions of animal behavior. Thus, he speaks of the vindictive rat, the salacious cock, the greedy vulture, the hypocritical cat and the lascivious dog. But no animal can be as depraved and intemperate as man, who has even lost his instinct for self-preservation. He pollutes the air he breathes, eats foods which shorten his life and often drinks himself to death. It is true that some animals, like the goat and the caterpillar, do not possess fastidious palates and that the camel is careless in his diet, often mistaking white stones for lumps of sugar. But these errors on the whole are not fatal. A so-called lower animal would have rejected the noxious apple that inflicted irreparable damage on Adam's digestive tract. Behaving like an animal may impair man's dignity but does not degrade him, for man shares with the animals only his body. The psalmist called himself a worm, a dead flea and a dog. Jerome referred to himself as a louse, *ego pulex*. But when the famous Italian theologian, Giulio Cesare Vanini, in the early seventeenth century suggested that man was a quadruped, he was arrested by the Inquisition and promptly burned after horrible tortures.

Nevertheless, man did not turn his back completely on his quondam companions, especially the ass and the vulture. He could not identify himself with them or wholly renounce them. In time his hostility turned to envy. Often, weary of his cerebral adventures, he would forget his linguistic preeminence and class consciousness and seek to be reunited with his dumb brethren. He secretly envied their unfallen state of innocence, their placid self-sufficiency, their unconscious vigor and speechless integrity. The longing of alienated man to return to the uncorrupted animal world is a common theme in modern literature and one that may be found in its most eminent representatives:

> I think I could turn and live with animals, they are so placid and
>   self-contain'd;
> I stand and look at them long and long.

They do not sweat and whine about their condition;
They do not lie awake in the dark and weep for their sins;
They do not make me sick discussing their duty to God;
Not one is dissatisfied—not one is demented with the mania of owning
 things;
Not one kneels to another, nor to his kind that lived thousands of years
 ago;
Not one is respectable or industrious over the whole earth.

—Walt Whitman, *Song of Myself,* 32

In the opening lines of his *Use and Abuse of History,* Nietzsche describes the placid life of the cow whose verminous existence is preferable to that of wretched man, for it eats and digests from morning to night without talking and is not tormented by feelings of guilt. To D.H. Lawrence the cow is also a symbol of salvation, for she lives simply and trusts her animal instincts; her blood, like her milk, flows without the impediment of mind, for she has no mind. Tolstoy in his *Kreutzer Sonata* (Chap. 16) envies the life of the hen who feeds and warms her chick, clucks for a while when it dies and then continues to live as before, trusting her instincts. In a similar vein Luther apostrophizes the sow, which he regards as a model of salvation: "For a sow lies in the gutter or on manure as if on the finest bed . . . and if the Turkish Caesar arrived in all his might and anger, the sow would be much too proud to move a single whisker in his honor . . . . The sow has not eaten from the apple, which in paradise has taught us wretched humans the difference between good and bad (quoted from E.H. Erikson, *Young Man Luther,* p. 30).

In his *Summer Impressions* (1862) Dostoyevski writes that he would readily give up his freedom for the life of a little ant on an ant-hill where "everything is so well-ordered, no one goes hungry and all are happy, everybody knows what he has to do; in fact, man has a long way to go before he can hope to reach the standards of an ant-hill."

Even the dog is envied for his superior wisdom, the theme of the "chien savant," as in E.T.A. Hoffmann's *Adventures of the Dog Berganza* (1814) and Baudelaire's *Les bon chiens.* It is the horse, however, that has dominated man's imagination from the earliest days. Man's affection for this noble animal has always been accompanied by great respect and often affection. A French poet, impressed by the prancing, stamping and rearing of horses, by their fragrant droppings and thunderous farts (for they live only on grass and air), found the anagram *heros* in the very name of "horse." The horse has provided us with a large variety of surnames, as illustrated in Chekov's charming story, *A Horsey Name*. The city of Stuttgart was originally "a garden for horses" *(Stuten-gart)*. In Tolstoy's short story, *Yardstick,* the world is seen from the standpoint of a horse. The greatest tribute to horses, however, comes from the hero of *Gulliver's Travels* (Chap. X), who found so much to admire in these mettlesome animals that he imitated their gestures, manners and gait and even learned their speech, which seemed to him similar to High Dutch or German.

Simianity vs. Humanity

Man's envy of the animals is not reciprocated. Animal lore contains many unflattering insights into man's condition. The general opinion in the animal world concerning man and his miserable existence has been best expressed by its most intelligent representatives, the apes, who stand next to man in order of creation. They had dreamed of man's coming for millennia, but when he finally appeared they were greatly disappointed, even annoyed. They found their simianity in no way inferior to his humanity. The superiority that man derived from his ability to speak was greatly exaggerated. Apes have also been known to speak when in a talking mood and not involved in arboreal distractions but have refrained from doing so lest they be mistaken for men. This voluntary silence has given them a reputation among animal psychologists as deep and cautious thinkers or mute philosophers.

Many animals have successfully resisted the attempts of linguistic anthropologists, who with their customary effrontery have looked down their throats (in case of the lion from outside the cage) in an effort to find the rudiments of human speech in the sounds with which the animal world regales us. Few animals are wholly silent, each having its own mode of expression: asses bray, moles rumble, doves moan, turtles weep, the monogamous rhinoceros yawns and the lovely elephant blows his trumpet; fish also emit amorous sounds too delicate for our dull ears to perceive. The repertory of animal sounds, however, is limited, devoid of variety and incapable of variation or improvement. The duck's dialect is confined to repetitive quacks, and the frog's inflections are today no different than in the days of Aristophanes. Animals are debarred from human articulation not because they are phonetically defective but because they are semantically blocked. It is true that the serpent's conversation in the Garden was marked by close reasoning and that Baalam's ass on one occasion outdid her master in repartee. But the serpent was soon deprived of the gift of speech for speaking falsely, and the ass never repeated her inspired performance. When an ass now speaks it is a miracle. Speech remains the sole criterion by which a human being can be distinguished. The story is told of a Spanish gentleman who, on hearing a parrot address him on his arrival in the New World, bowed deeply and said: "Pardon, your Excellency, but I thought you were a bird."

The simian view of man has come down to us in a number of documents. The earliest of these is in the form of a letter written in Sumerian by a monkey to his mother around the year 2000 B.C. in which he complains of the harsh life and miserable food in the prosperous city of Ur where he was living in the house of a master musician, and he begs his mother to send a messenger to rescue him from his intolerable human environment. This rare "Monkey Letter," which had been preserved by Sumerian scribes, has been translated into English and placed at my disposal by Prof. Aaron Shaffer of the Hebrew University in Jerusalem.

The second document is likewise in the form of a letter written by a more sophisticated ape, known as César de Malaca, the offspring of a woman of Malaca and a baboon. That apes raped black women was a common notion at the beginning of the last century, and was even believed by Thomas Jefferson (cf. *Notes on Virginia, Query 14*). This ape had been brought up in human society under the tutelage of a respect-

III.ᵉ Vol. 18   *Lettre d'un Singe*

Cesar de Malaca, écrivant aux Animaux de Son espéce.

able lady. The ape's letter is addressed to the members of his own species and was published at the end of the eighteenth century in the posthumous works of Restif de la Bretonne, an enlightened social philosopher who was popularly known as "the Rousseau of the gutter," under the title: *Lettre d'un singe aux êtres de son espèce* (Leipzig, 1781, III, p. 19ff).[1] In the illustration that faces the letter (see facing page) an ape dressed as a gentleman, seated at a desk with a manuscript before him, holding a pen in his mouth and resting his head on one hand, evidently in profound meditation. In his letter the simian author relates his experiences as a member of the human race, the miseries and torments of human existence, and warns his former fellow-apes not to follow his example but to remain as they are—apes, bears, dogs, cats, anything but that vile creature man, with his hypocrisy, sentimentality and greed, and with his proud reason which is the chief cause of his endless follies. In conclusion he bids his erstwhile companions adieu, imploring them never to surrender their birthright of "salut, repos, bonne-nourriture, liberté . . . et ignorance sempiternelle."

The third simian document that provides us with an unflattering view of human nature is an account of an interview granted by a former ape, now called Herr Kopeter, to a distinguished member of a German learned society. This interview was faithfully transcribed and published by Franz Kafka in his *Collected Works* under the title: "A Report to an Academy." The former ape relates how he was wounded in the thigh on being captured, and offers to pull down his breeches so that the interviewer might see the scars of the hidden wound with his own eyes. He goes on to speak of his early struggles to overcome his simian nature and of his efforts to acquire human characteristics— how he learned to smoke and drink, to reason and deceive, and how he finally became neurotic and had to be sent to a sanatorium to convalesce. No self-respecting animal in its right mind, he concludes,

---

[1]Restif's life was marked by many eccentricities, including a passion for pretty female shoes which he is said to have contracted as a child when, crawling about the floor, he lifted up a little girl's petticoat by chance and encountered a soft slipper, whereupon a whipping followed which determined a permanent fixation.

would, of its own volition, possibly desire to become a member of human society.

As the world became more and more impenetrable to human reason, writers arose who urged men to renounce their spiritual superiority not only to the animal kingdom but to the world of things. It is time we put an end to our pretence of a supernatural status over against the rest of God's creation and stopped strutting about as independent thinkers: *cogito ergo sum*. The hypocritical human spirit must be deflated to its literal meaning of "wind," to belching, snoring and farting: *La vida es un pedo*. An audacious attempt to abandon man's egocentric rationality and return to the wisdom of the senses is recorded by William Burroughs in his novel *Naked Lunch* where he recounts the story of a man who taught his anus to take over the functions of the mouth, especially speech, to imitate its grimaces, its pursed lips (for kissing), its windy mouthings and back talk. The faculty of speech that had lifted man above the tongue-tied brutes was now assumed by the most despised part of the human frame to remind man that he was nothing but an empty windbag, a talking anus.

The world is not our private property and we have no right to inflict meaning on its things and ride roughshod over them with our preconceived ideas. Away with prosopopeia and tapinosis![2] Let us cease our struggle with mechanical gadgets, revolving doors, bottle openers, shoelaces, corkscrews, hats in the wind, misplaced eyeglasses—with the silent poltergeist that is imbued with a spirit of revenge and with a sense of humor that we fail to appreciate.[3] Let us make our peace with the

---

[2]*Prosopopeia* in another name for the so-called pathetic fallacy which attributes human qualities to inanimate things. *Tapinosis* is a figure of speech that diminishes the worth of a human quality by comparing it with an inanimate object, as when a person is called "a stuffed shirt" or "windbag"; an example of a bold tapinosis is Pope's daring line: "And Maids turn'd Bottles, called aloud for Corks" *(The Rape of the Lock)*.

[3]For which we have the apt German expression *Tücke des Objekts*, the cussedness of things, coined by Friedrich Theodor Vischer. In his popular novel *Auch Einer* (1878), the hero is constantly thwarted by inanimate objects. "There are few moments in a man's existence when he experiences so much ludicrous distress, or meets with so little

world of things, not the meretricious advertised products that whisper in our ear "Buy me (on installments), I'm cheap, I'll rescue you from loneliness," and attend to things in their "sensational nudity" (William James), detached from the word, even as Adam saw them in Eden before giving them names.

Three writers, all active in the first half of this century, devoted themselves almost exclusively to rescuing the world of things from obscurity. Francis Ponge in his many works, especially in *Opting for Things,* gives us brief insights into the life of common things: oysters, peacocks, raindrops, pebbles—things we fail to notice in our hurried existence. Karel Čapek, the Czech writer who coined the word *robot,* allows things to speak for themselves with detached irony (e.g., in his *Fables*)—a match: I am the eternal flame; a mirror: the world is nothing but my idea, and outside me there is nothing; a pole in a fence: look at that stupid tree, nothing but branches and disorder. The most gifted of these so-called "chosist" writers was the native Spaniard, Ramón Gómez de la Serna, who became renowned for his creation of the literary form which he called *greguarías,* whimsical observations of familiar things seen in an unfamiliar light, sometimes accompanied by an illustration—for example: lightning is a kind of enraged corkscrew; hothouses are model prisons for plants; a snail is always going up its own spiral staircase; a siphon is water with a hiccup. The concern of these writers with the common things around them *(chosism)* coincided with the rise of the phenomenological movement in the days before the First World War. The watchword of this movement was that of its central and most influential figure, Edmund Husserl: *Zu den Sachen,* to the things themselves, an exhortation to look at phenomena and describe them as faithfully as possible, free of theoretical commitments and unexamined assumptions.

The disillusion among writers and philosophers at the turn of the

---

charitable commiseration, as when in pursuit of his own hat." (Dickens, *Pickwick Papers,* IV).

century in the power of reason and human speech gave rise to a widespread fascination for inanimate puppets and dolls whose wooden wisdom is not the faltering logic of the mind and confusions of human speech but the remote beauty of geometric relations. This subject gave rise to an extensive literature, inspired by Heinrich von Kleist's brief but highly influential essay written at the end of the eighteenth century, *The Marionette Theater,* which is one of the literary treasures of the German-speaking people. The Austrian poet, Rainer Maria Rilke, retained a lifelong interest in dolls, having been brought up by his parents as a girl until the age of nine. The English poet, Francis Thompson, wrote an essay called *The Fourth Estate of Humanity,* in which he describes the doll as the crown of creation nearest to the life of the quiet gods, with its painted face, counterfeit lashes, alien hair and false bosom, the condition to which all women aspire.

This widespread interest in the puppet at the beginning of the new century deeply affected the life of the theater, mainly through the dramatic theories of Gordon Craig *(On the Art of the Theater).* The human body, as he discovered after many years of acting, was a poor instrument for dramatic representation, pampered by passions it does not feel, at the mercy of irresistible sneezes, eructations and sudden itches that demand immediate attention. A new form of acting must be created based on the symbolic gestures of the puppet, who is content to serve the poet in silence. Oscar Wilde spoke admiringly of puppets after seeing them perform in Shakespeare's *Tempest:*

> There are many advantages in puppets. They never argue. They have no crude views about art. They have no private lives. We are never bothered by accounts of their virtues, or bored by recitals of their vices; and when they are out of an engagement they never do good in public or save people from drowning, nor do they speak more than is set down for them. They recognize the presiding intellect of the dramatist, and have never been known to ask for their parts to be written up. They are admirably docile, and have no personalities at all . . . . Their gestures were quite sufficient, and the words that seemed to come from their little lips were spoken by poets who had beautiful voices. It was a delightful per-

formance, and I remember it still with delight, though Miranda took no notice of the flowers I sent her after the curtain fell.

(Quoted in Pearson, H., *The Life of Oscar Wilde,* Penguin, 1960, p. 222)

IX

Words as Weapons

A GOOD PART OF OUR LIVES IS TAKEN UP WITH VERBAL ABUSE, ANGRY disputes, recrimination, bickering and bitchery, name calling, *tu quoque* (you're another!), flyting. Flyting is an old word that refers to the bragging and taunts (sometimes in poetical form) exchanged by combatants as prelude to a contest, such as those between David and Goliath or between Kissarse and Bumfondle in Rabelais' *Pantagruel* (Chaps. 11-13). Flyting is roughly equivalent to the transitive verb "to bad-mouth," referring to the stream of abuse often used by boxers to distract and upset their opponents. The literary and learned world is not exempt from this unpleasant side of our nature and has at its disposal a whole arsenal of fine invective: disparaging epithets, corrosive wit, lethal barbs and malicious *bon mots,* a classical example of which is Alexander Pope's venomous passage on Sporus, Lord Derby, in his *Epistle to Dr. Arbuthnot.* The verbal aggressiveness of literary men may stem in part from their lack of real power and their consequent overestimation of the punitive force of words: *Lengua sin manos, cómo osas hablar* / Tongue without hands, how dare you speak (El Cid). Nor is the hankering after altercation absent from the warm atmosphere of conjugal life where intimacy renders it more malignant.

We hardly feel the crushing force of the punitive gestures that lurk in the original meaning of *insult* to leap upon, *retort* to twist back, *rebuke* to strike with a club, *debate* to beat down, *discuss* to dash to bits, *sarcasm* a tearing of the flesh, *haste* violent struggle, *repartee* ready to return a blow (cf. Ger. *schlagfertig* quick-witted, lit. prepared to deliver a blow). We are ordinarily hardly conscious of the deep hostility and wounding force concealed in these half-hidden gestures:

> And all that silent language which so oft
> In conversation between man and man
> Blots out from the human countenance all trace
> Of beauty and of love.
> —Wordsworth, *The Prelude,* II.457-460

These aggressive gestures are normally concealed or disguised[1] but can be swiftly mobilized and be given free rein as soon as social restraints are relaxed. Men can be persuaded to kill their fellowmen provided they are given the proper slogans that absolve them from moral responsibility and silence the demands of critical reason. In Dürrenmatt's play, *The Visit of the Old Lady,* a wealthy woman is able to persuade the law-abiding citizens of a Swiss town to kill one of their neighbors who had jilted her many years ago and ruined her life. The good burghers are at first shocked at her proposal but, yielding to cajolery, bribes, appeals to justice and veiled threats, finally assent. On a larger scale these aggressive gestures that generally remain below the surface are released in there current wars that afflict mankind. Wars are games in which men are killed by battalions of slogans (Ger. *Schlag-*

---

[1]This is the region that the French novelist, Natalie Sarraute, has made her own and explained as "tropisms" (also called *sarrauteries*), the region of repressed gestures, venemous glances and silent acrimony in the hinterland of thought before words reach conscious articulation. Another consummate master of the sly look and secret glance that express the subtle relations between people is Thomas Hardy, who spies on his characters as they spy on each other.

wörter, lit. words that deal blows) and die not from bullets but from verbal wounds.[2] This was a common theory of the origin of wars, especially in the period of disillusion and weariness that followed World War I.

An extreme example of a word that kills *literally* may be found in Ionescu's play *The Lesson,* in which a teacher of languages defines the word "knife" by plunging a real knife into the heart of one of his students, a striking instance of the direct method of learning by experience. A more conventional method would have been simply to repeat the dictionary definition of "knife" as "an instrument that cuts," which indicates its specific characteristic, for "knife" (just as Fr. *couteau,* Arab. *sakina,* Rus. *nozh*) is not an object that is found in the external world but a pure linguistic fact defined in the dictionary. Even one who is familiar with the different uses of a knife will not know the meaning of "knife" unless he knows the meaning assigned to it in the English dictionary. Conversely, one who has never used a knife will readily understand the dictionary definition, although not every cutting instrument is a knife (e.g., scissors, razor, guillotine) nor can a knife be used to cut metal, stone, glass, wood or such non-cuttable things as air or water, except in an absurd or metaphorical sense.

The teacher in Ionescu's play, however, was determined to reverse the traditional subordination of things to words and to define the word "knife" by inscribing it in the very heart of the unfortunate student. With this daring leap beyond the confines of language he liberated the object from its subservience to verbal meaning and human involvement, thus closing the gap between nature and spirit and realizing the age-old dream of philosophers and poets, namely, the creation of a language whose words can break skulls. The sensational method adopted by the French teacher must nevertheless be judged morally obtuse and vicious and subversive of all sound pedagogical principles, for he failed to give the poor student the opportunity to defend herself against the practical consequences of an untried linguistic theory—a theory, moreover, that

---

[2]This is the theme of Boris Vian's moving drama *Le gouter des generaux.*

could have been illustrated with a blunter object, such as a shoehorn or bottle opener. In *Evenings on a Farm near Dikanko,* Gogol tells the story of a schoolboy who forgot the name for a garden rake. While working in the garden, he accidentally stepped on the teeth of the rake so that the handle, swinging upward, cracked him on the forehead, whereupon the boy yelled: "Damn rake." Thus, the rake itself instantly drove home to the boy's memory the knowledge of its name.

Nevertheless, the direct method of defining an object described above is in some respects superior to purely verbal definitions which often defeat genuine comprehension. A verbal definition, however strict, is still subject to endless interpretations and disputes, as we know from the history of dogmatics and the rise of religious schisms. Initial definitions do not exhaust the significance of a word. The meaning of a word emerges from the different contexts in which it is used *during* discussion, which often turns out to be altogether different from what had been originally intended. Entire works have been based on the progressive elaboration of the words of the title which gathers up meaning as the plot develops. In more than forty of his plays, Lope de Vega takes a proverb for the title whose unsuspected meanings gradually emerge during the course of the play. In Goncharev's novel *The Precipice,* the author describes a meeting of lovers at the edge of a precipice, their precipitous elopement, headlong flight, rash decisions. Gogol, in his short story *The Nose,* develops the various meanings of Russian "nosological" idioms as the plot unfolds in the course of the story: to follow one's nose, thumb one's nose, go off with a long nose (to be peeved), look down one's nose, to be nosey.

We all know tedious pedants who cry "Define your terms!" and who insist that the best way to resolve an argument is to define in advance the terms on which the disagreement depends. It is assumed that a precise, logical definition is equivalent to precise thinking, which is seldom the case. Gradgrind, the schoolmaster in Dickens' *Hard Times,* demands of his students definitions based on facts:

Now, what I want is, Facts. Teach these boys and girls nothing but Facts. Facts are wanted in life. Plant nothing else, and root out everything else.

You can only form the minds of reasoning animals upon Facts; nothing else will ever be of any service to them. This is the principle on which I bring up these children. Stick to the Facts, sir! . . . In this life we want nothing but Facts; nothing but Facts!.

"Blitzer," said Thomas Gradgrind, "your definition of a horse."

"Quadruped. Graminivorous. Forty teeth, namely twenty-four grinders, four eye-teeth, and twelve incisive. Sheds coat in the spring; in marshy countries, sheds hoofs, too. Hoofs hard, but requiring to be shod with iron. Age known by marks in the mouth."

"Now girl number twenty," said Mr. Gradgrind. "You know what a horse is?"

Girl number twenty, however, was unable to come up with a definition of a horse, although she had spent her whole life among horses and among people whose livelihood depended on a real knowledge of horses and knew them well. This calculating philosophy of Gradgrindery is directed by Dickens against Bentham, the father of utilitarianism, the philosophy that measures happiness quantitatively by numbers, intensity and duration and ignores the life of the imagination and the emotions. Gradgrind's insistence on factual definitions is often calculated to forestall discussion and obstruct the free expression of unpopular ideas and in the hands of the learned takes the form of verbal bullying to cudgel uneducated or shy folk into acquiesence, of which the best-known example is the Squire's silencing of Moses in Oliver Goldsmith's *The Vicar of Wakefield* (Chap. 7):

—"Very well," cried the 'Squire, speaking very quick, "the premises being thus settled, I proceed to observe, that the concatanation of self existences, proceeding in a reciprocal duplicate ratio, naturally produce a problematical dialogism, which in some measure proves that the essence of spirituality may be referred to the second predictable"—"Hold, hold," cried the other, "I deny that: Do you think I can thus tamely submit to such heterodox doctrines?"—"What," replied the 'Squire, as if in a passion, "not submit! Answer me one plain question: Do you think Aristotle right when he says, that relatives are related?" "Undoubtedly," replied the other.—"If so then," cried the 'Squire, "answer me directly to what I propose: Whether do you judge the analytical investigation of the first part of my enthymem deficient secundum quoad, or quoad minus, and give me your reasons: give me your reasons, I say, directly."—"I protest," cried Moses, "I don't rightly comprehend the force of your reasoning; but if it be reduced to one simple proposition, I fancy it may then have an answer."—"O, sir," cried the 'Squire, "I am your most humble servant, I find you want me to furnish you with argument and intellects too. No, sir, there I protest you are too hard for me." This effectually raised the laugh against poor Moses, who sate the only dismal figure in a groupe of merry faces: nor did he offer a single syllable more during the whole entertainment.

Gradgrind's pedagogic principle, "Don't think, memorize facts!" rests on the assumption that understanding will come later with maturity and experience. Another more recent school of pedagogy, however, insists that facts are useless altogether and cannot be trusted to reflect the complexity of human experience. Cultivate opinions instead of facts and express them with conviction! The student thus becomes opinionated, argumentative and intolerant and learns to cheat with words. Our appreciation of general truths, the argument runs, is not dependent on their accurate formulation in factual definitions. Our appreciation of beauty, goodness, freedom or the colors of the rainbow cannot be made intelligible to one who is not already aware of them. We know many things intuitively although we cannot articulate our knowledge in words. "I know what time is," St. Augustine writes, "but if someone asks me what it is I cannot answer and it then seems to me that I do not know." A poet derives little benefit from the acquisition of knowledge. Keats' well-known principle of "negative capability" advises poets to cultivate ignorance, to clear the mind of conventional knowledge and the irritable pursuit of facts and make it a thoroughfare for unanticipated thoughts. "I am an ignorant man," Santayana confessed, "almost a poet."[3]

---

[3]Cf. also Keats' *Cave of Quietude,* the oxymoronic den of happy gloom, dark Paradise and articulate silence; also Blake's married land of Beulah, the poet's refuge from perpetual mental activity and the fury of creation.

Ignorance may be the privilege of tender-minded philosophers and poets, but we find it also recommended to historians who are urged to beware of factual knowledge that confuses and obscures the vision of the whole and to present the past in the form of interesting dialogue, colorful scenes and animated portraiture: "For ignorance is the first requisite of the historian—ignorance which simplifies and clarifies, which selects and omits, with a placid perfection unattainable by the highest art" (Lytton Strachey, *Eminent Victorians*, Preface). Literary historians (e.g., Carlyle, Macaulay, Trevelyan in England, Bancroft, Motley, Parkaman in America) seek to recreate the events of a bygone age, to describe the daily life of the masses, the joys and sorrows of domestic life, styles of dress and architecture, the foibles and intrigues of their rulers. To this end facts are selected and arranged, not with an eye to historical truth but in accordance with a preconceived pattern or intense vision whose aim is to instruct and inspire, which makes for a didactic, anecdotal and dramatic style that often borders on fiction. The notion that creative thinking is the result of a dispassionate study of objective facts, even in scientific work, is a myth. "It is not the clear-sighted who lead the world. Great achievements are accomplished in a blessed warm mental fog" (Conrad).

Etymologies, both real and fanciful, have also been used for polemical purposes by learned people, ostensibly to find a common ground of agreement prior to the discussion of a controversial subject. Tendentious etymologies were formerly widely employed, by Ruskin, Carlyle, Emerson, Cardinal Newman and others, to point an argument or support a disputed truth. Such corroborations, however, were seldom convincing and only served to bring etymologizing into disrepute. Thus, vegetarianism was recommended because of its root meaning, Lat. *vegetare* to enliven, quicken (although "to vegetate" has acquired a directly opposite meaning, namely, to lead an inactive life); "to be human" was taken to mean to be rooted to the earth and to the life of the senses (Lat. *humus* earth). During the Middle Ages woman's inferior position was confirmed by deriving "virgin" from Lat. *vir* man + *gin* trap; Ger. *Weib* woman, from *weben* to weave (lies); "feminine" from *fe* faith + *minus* little, to indicate woman's feeble religious impulses. In his autobiographical study Freud relates how his work on hysteria was impeded because of the widely accepted derivation of "hysteria" from the Greek word for womb.

Against these learned polemical weapons, simple folk have no defense except the use of the proverb (cf. Sancho Panza in his disputes with Don Quixote), a practice now falling into disuse even in Spain where peasants were formerly noted for their sententiousness. The proverb is the common place of accepted social values and habits where all men meet on equal terms; it provides us with ready-made truths that could be repeated without reflection or critical analysis. To quote a proverb of long-established authority is a safer weapon in dispute than hazarding an independent judgment. Hence, it is not surprising that radical critics—William Blake, Bertold Brecht, John Dos Passos and Francis Ponge, among others—have singled out this seemingly innocent genre as the most inauthentic mode of speech. The proverb is to be distrusted as a vehicle of unexamined social prejudices. Its very persuasiveness and appeal to common sense, its alliterative folk wisdom, often cast in the imperative mood, led Nietzsche to assume that the proverb was the invention of the dominant class, designed to impose a conventional morality on the gullible masses. It is folly to believe that proverbial wisdom stems from or resides in the masses whose principal characteristics are self-interest, ignorance and sentimentality: *vox populi vox dei* / the masses are asses.

Vocal language did not arise because of man's need for social intercourse and mutual understanding, as is generally assumed, but because some men, chiefly rogues, discovered that voice was better adapted than gestures to cajole and hoodwink the masses and convince them that might is right, menial work noble, honesty the best policy, private property sacred. Men, like rabbits, as Mirabeau observed, are caught by their ears. The very act of naming implies ownership. When man first named the sheep *bah-bah*, in imitation of the sound it emitted, he therewith proclaimed: "You belong to me, your wool is mine; what I cannot use I'll hoard and sell at a profit; the more I accumulate the more I am: *habeo ergo sum.*" Here we have the origin of our predatory society, the pattern of all the conquests and usurpations in human history. The analogy of property and language was given a more favorable interpretation by Auguste Comte, the philosopher of positivism, who regarded them as the two agents of civilization whereby material goods accumulated by the active will as property, on the one hand, and human culture accumulated by the intelligence as language, on the other, are preserved and transmitted from generation to generation. Unlike the utopian reformers who look forward to an egalitarian society of the future, Comte turns to the past, grateful to our acquisitive ancestors for the material property and linguistic culture they bequeathed to us, the bond that unites us in one continuous humanity.

Onomastic Malice and Malaise

The ancients were not squeamish about their names: Oedipus *swell-foot*, Boccaccio *big-mouth*, Varus *bowlegs*, Crassus *fatty*, Cicero *chick-pea*, because of an unpleasant excrescence on the orator's nose at birth. The name Jacob means "heel" literally, for the patriarch emerged from the womb holding on to Esau's heel, and also in the slang sense of "deceiver," for having dished his brother out of his birthright with a pot of lentil soup. The biblical addiction to name-punning is widespread among literary men. Thomas Hood, the most prolific of English punsters, could not resist making his last pun: "Now the undertaker will earn (urn) a liveli*hood.*" Schleiermacher, *veil-maker,* is an apt name for the father of modern hermeneutics, as is Feuerbach, "the *fiery brook* that must be crossed" (Karl Marx).

The distortion of names is generally inspired by malice and intended to harm the owner of the name. Metternich's name was sometimes written *Milli-Metter*nich to cut him down to size; the pretender to the Austrian throne was called by the English *Perhaps*burg; Proust was lengthened to *Proustitute,* and T. Eliot written in reverse as *Toilet;* Walt Whitman's followers were called *Whitmaniacs,* and Chagall called the *jackal* of modern painting; Luther wrote the name of his enemy, Dr. Eck, as one word (*Dreck* filth) and that of Thomas Murner as Murr-

Narr (growl-fool). Similarly, we have distortions such as Ibsenity, Buberonics, Lisztless, Kafkastrophic, Dusty Evsky.[4] James Joyce was fond of distorting historical names: Suffoclose (Sophocles), Daunty and Gouty (Dante and Goethe), Bottom-Silly (Botticelli), Hug-arse (Hogarth). Some names lend themselves to distortion: Disraeli was known to his friends as Dizzy, John Keats as Junkets, and Stirling Coyne as Filthy Lucre.[5] Freud was aware of the practical effect of such associations and suggested that movie stars might profitably adopt names that lend themselves to somewhat lewd or erotic interpretations, perhaps such names as Fanny Bottome, Peabody Wetmore, Gregory Philpot, Café O'Lay, the famous Harlem beauty, Joshua Longbottom (alluding to *ars longa, vita brevis*) or Adolph Bouguereau, the name of the sentimental French painter to which Oscar Wilde is said to have been partial (oh, bugger, oh!).

Writers of a rationalistic turn of mind regard proper names as arbitrary designations, meaningless marks which in no way indicate the attributes of the bearer. An extreme instance of this attitude is that of Diodorus, the ancient Greek who called his slaves by the names of the Greek particles. We tend to read into names our subjective preferences and associations. Does fame love only high-sounding names? Did Wellington conquer India because of his resonant name? Is Kosciusko less admired than Mirabeau? Is Klopstock too dull a name to vie with that of Milton? Is the name of Baron de Rothschild uttered with more

---

[4]That the name of Duns Scotus should have come down to us as *dunce* is a grave injustice to the memory of the celebrated scholastic theologian of the thirteenth century who was one of the keenest minds of his age.

[5]Proper names made the butt of innocent raillery are to be found in the so-called *clerihew,* named after Edmund Clerihew Bentley, who was addicted to this form of nonsense verse, the best known of which is: Sir Humphrey Davy/ Detested gravy,/ He lived in the odium/ Of having invented sodium. The clerihew differs from the limerick in that it uses real and not fictitious names and is not obscene so that the last line need not be mumbled. The jiggery-pokery, the most notable invention of its kind since the clerihew, is a somewhat more complex form, consisting of two quatrains, the last line of the first rhyming with the last line of the second, all other lines being composed of two dactyls; the first line is a nonsense line, the second a proper name, and at least one of the subsequent lines only one word long.

reverence than that of Jamsetjee Jeejeebhoy, the great Indian philan-
thropist who died in Bombay in 1859? Did Danton and Robespierre
fare any better than Anarcharis Clootz, the French patriot who was
guillotined at the same time?

Men seem to have a strong desire to immortalize their names. The
herostratic or counterrevolutionary sense of a word, often used by
Lenin's followers, is an historical allusion to Herostratus, a Greek
incendiary who burned down the Temple of Diana in 356 B.C. in order
to achieve fame and make his name immortal. To defeat his intention
the Ephesians forbade his name ever to be mentioned. Absalom, who
burned Joab's corn, was a herostratist. The Turkish proverb about
urinating in the well of Zamzam, the sacred well of Mecca—a monstrous deed even for a Turk—is a herostratic act. A strange instance of
herostratism is provided by a famous Italian astrologer of the sixteenth
century who, having prognosticated the day of his death, committed
suicide on that very day so as to maintain his reputation as an astrologer.
A strong herostratic impulse is evident in our contemporary terrorists
who pursue their deeds at a high cost. Notoriety is preferable to
obscurity and oblivion: *Muero yo, viva mi fama* / Death is bitter, but
fame eternal. We all long for the taste of fame and the approbation
of history, although we may no longer be here to enjoy it: "Even
philosophers who write books despising glory place their names on the
title page" (Spinoza). Prudence, not modesty, keeps the herostratic hero
from boasting about his exploits. However, he cannot endure prolonged anonymity and often contrives to get himself caught by acts of
deliberate carelessness. When Herostratus was executed it was forbid-
den to mention his name on pain of death. Yet his name endures, while
the names of the architects of the temple are lost in oblivion. Infamy
is also fame.

Language as an Instrument of Deception

Human speech is by its very nature ambiguous and imprecise and
thus ideally suited for misrepresentation, dissimulation, equivocation
and sophistry. Our language thinks for us and also lies for us. Verbal

deception is coeval with the earliest lispings of the race and was already practiced in the Garden of Eden, especially by the serpent, whose sloughed-off skin, split tongue and *strabismus divergens* are still the ophidian signs of divine punishment and the universal symbols of falsehood. Prevarication, or the deliberate intent to deceive, is no longer found among animals, except in a few birds who employ feints or ruses designed to mislead. All men, however, are liars (Ps. 115:1), (Pa. 116:11). The patriarch Jacob was a notorious liar, although his recorded deception is described by St. Augustine, the first Western thinker to make lying the subject of philosophical speculation, not as a lie but as a mystery: *non est mendacium sed mysterium.*

Most of our numerous daily lies are not regarded as perjurious or morally reprehensible and no blemish is attached to them: the "white lies" that preserve the humaneness of social relations, the "noble lies" in the interest of the state (Plato) or of the classless society of the future (Lenin), the monstrous lies of writers of commercials, the gigantic lies of cooks and fishermen, the charitable untruths of the mother of an unmarried girl, the lies of children (who develop the capacity for lying at an early age with astonishing rapidity), the inventive mendacity of malingerers to simulate insanity (paralogia or the Ganser syndrome) and, not least, the flattering lies of lovers: "Therefore I lie with her and she with me" (Shakespeare, *Sonnets,* 138). People expect to be lied to and are disconcerted by a consistent adherence to the truth. Grillparzer's drama *Woe to Him Who Lies,* in which the hero gains his ends by invariably telling the truth, failed to meet with public approval in his native Austria. The propensity for lying is widespread, and it is surprising that people are still found who earnestly seek the truth and are even willing to give their lives for it—*vitam impendere vero* (Lucretius)— confident that it will ultimately bear away the victory. This is all the more surprising since the pursuit of truth does not seem to be native to the human mind. Most people are not strong enough to live with the unadulterated truth. In his novel *The Idiot,* Dostoyeveski describes the discomfiture of the participants in a parlor game when asked to recount some shameful incident in their lives without lying. People disguise the truth for a number of reasons, out of ignorance, deviousness, self-deception or fear. Yet we all proceed on the assumption that what we hear or read is trustworthy and bears the character of plausibility until we learn otherwise (cf. the boy who cried "Wolf!"). Plausibility is greatest where language is most standardized and institutionalized and rests on an accepted moral code. The literature of the late nineteenth century, for example, is filled with the tall stories, exaggerations and equivocations of charlatans, quacks, confidence men and mountebanks, for it was an age of uncertain ethical values which tolerated a good deal of cant and humbug.

Kant's moral imperative that requires us to tell the truth under all circumstances regardless of the consequences is not a reliable guide in situations where the perplexed conscience is faced with conflicting duties. Hugo Grotius, the renowned Dutch jurist and legal philosopher, was of the opinion that parents have the right to lie to their children. The Talmud makes three exceptions to the rule of truth: we are not bound to tell the truth in matters concerning marital relations; a scholar, out of modesty and to avoid a show of learning, may deny familiarity with a talmudic tractate; and a guest may be untruthful concerning the generosity of his host so as not to encourage unwelcome visitors. Goethe seems to have agreed with Plato that a sovereign may lie and deceive for the benefit of the state, but the ruled must tell the truth, for he repeated to Eckermann with approval the old Latin proverb: *Qui nescit dissimilare nescit regnare* / A ruler who does not break his word when circumstances compel him to do so is not fit to rule. There is nevertheless a universal intuitive repugnancy against lying. We feel that lying is not only bad but wrong since it implies a deliberate intention to manipulate the mind of another human being on a concealed unilateral principle. Truth is not one's personal property, and to tamper with it is a social offense. Every lie is a promise made and broken at the same time and thus undermines our trust in language as a means of social communication.

We lie for many different reasons, but we do not defend lying on principle. This was done, for example, by the gifted Russian anarchist and aphorist, V. Rozanov, one of the foremost representatives of the formalist movement, who believed the lie to be an indispensable ingredient in the construction of reality and openly defended the right to lie *on principle* against an unjust and hypocritical society:

> It is surprising how I managed to accommodate myself to falsehood. And for this odd reason: what business is it of yours what precisely I think? Why am I obliged to tell you my real thoughts? . . . I have gone through my whole life as though behind a curtain that is immovable, untearable. Nobody dares touch that curtain. There I live, there with myself I was truthful. . . . and it seemed to me that no one had anything to do with the truth of anything I said on the other side of the curtain.

Although Rozanov was vigorously attacked by his contemporaries, including Trotsky, he had only adopted in his personal life a social theory that had been made respectable by a distinguished German professor of that period, Hans Vaihinger, the author of *The Philosophy "As If."* According to this theory, man needs to supplement reality by an ideal world of auxiliary constructions of fictions that are acknowledged as false but which are of great practical importance in coping with the world, such fictions as conscience, social contract, the Virgin birth, the kingdom of God. Unlike Rozanov's lies, however, these fictions are adopted in the public interest and generally regarded as beneficial. The arguments given by Rozanov in favor of lying—that it leads to the truth, makes life more tolerable and is no different from the imaginative fiction of poets and historians—are also found in verse form in Browning's *Mr. Sludge, the Medium.* In a light-hearted mood, Oscar Wilde explained that the materialism and indifference to poetic ideals among the Americans are the result of having adopted as their national hero a man who, according to his own confession, was incapable of telling a lie. Although the story of George Washington and the cherry tree is a pure myth, it has done incalculable harm to the American imagination.

Every profound thinker needs a curtain, like Rozanov, a mask behind which he can be true to himself. Descartes, the exponent of philosophical clarity, lived his secret life under the motto *Larvatus prodeo* /Masked I advance. The sentimental author of works on child education, Rousseau, consigned his five illegitimate children to a foundling home. Richard Wagner, who extolled the virtues of chastity and vegetarianism, indulged in one sex affair after another and never gave up his French cuisine. James Fenimore Cooper wrote admiringly of the rough life of the pioneers in the American wilderness from a safe distance in Paris where he lived in the finest hotels hobnobbing with royalty. The timid scholar, Walter Pater, glorified the dangerous life but recoiled from the prospect of matrimony. Although himself "a child of disbelief and doubt," Dostoyevski preached the orthodox faith so as to spare the common folk the unbearable suffering that comes from the knowledge of the truth. Frederick the Great in his *Anti-Machiavelli* expresses his abhorrence of cruelty, treachery, perfidy and rapacity, characteristics for which he became notorious, thus proving to be an apt pupil of Machiavelli, his book serving as a mask behind which he could practice the vices he inveighed against. In his *Life of Kant*, Stuckenberg recounts that when the great moral philosopher received the news that the vessel bearing his favorite fruits had been delayed by a storm and that the members of the crew, finding themselves short of provisions, were compelled to consume the delicacies destined for him, he was greatly annoyed and declared that they should have starved rather than violate the categorical imperative. But as Kant himself observed in *An Idea for a Universal History:* "Even philosophers, wise though they are believed to be, are not wise enough to plan their own lives and live according to the rules they have made for themselves."

Kant himself, when admonished by Frederick William in 1794 to cease his subversive writing against the state and religion, submissively promised obedience, following Luther, who urged Christians to obey the orders of authority. The hasty accommodation of the great ethical philosopher was applauded by the enemies of the Enlightenment and set a bad example for later generations of Germans. When confronted with reality, Kant qualified his own high-minded moral principle that "a man's moral action must be taken irrespective of its end or consequence" by introducing a distinction between sincerity *(Aufrichtigkeit)* and candor *(Offenherzigkeit)* which he explained in a letter to Moses Mendelssohn as follows: "I think many things with the clearest conviction which I have not the courage to say. But I will never say anything I do not think." Although this distinction does not involve direct lying, it leaves room for tacit misrepresentation by concealing the truth.

We admire the great men of our race, its intellectual heroes and saints, and are surprised to discover on closer acquaintance that, apart from their singular gifts, they are often disfigured by petty traits of selfishness, envy and inordinate vanity. The early Greeks believed that there was an obvious correspondence between a man's outer appearance and his inner character: the handsome and intelligent Odysseus outwits the ugly and cruel Cyclops. The Greek word for ugly *aischros* thus came to mean "bad," and the word for beautiful *kalos* acquired the meaning of "good." Before the end of fifth century, however, a new realism emerged as a result of bitter experience, and the Greeks became conscious of the deceptiveness of this naive correspondence. The good and bad were found to be curiously mixed in the human psyche and difficult to disentangle. The ugly Socrates could now be regarded as having a beautiful personality, and frail Demosthenes as having a strong character. In time it was realized that what appear to be vices might be the fertile soil in which virtues flourish, so that to eradicate the one would also destroy the other:

> Take from LUTHER his roughness and fiery courage; from CALVIN his hectic obstinancy; from ERASMUS his timid prudence; hypocrisy and fanaticism from CROMWELL; from HENRY IV his sanguine character; mysticism from FENELON; from HUME his all-unhinging wit; love of paradox and brooding suspicion from ROUSSEAU; naïvetè and elegance of knavery from VOLTAIRE; from MILTON the extravagance of his all-personifying fancy; from RAFAELLE his dryness and nearly hard precision; and from RUBENS his supernatural luxury of colours:—deduct this oppressive EXUBERANCE from each; rectify them according to your own taste—what will be the result? your own correct, pretty, flat, useful—for me, to be sure, quite convenient vulgarity.

And why this amongst maxims of humanity? that you may learn to know this EXUBERANCE, this LEVEN, of each great character, and its effects on contemporaries and posterity—. . . .

(William Blake, *Annotations to Lavater*)

X

The Renunciation of Language

A LONG AND POWERFUL TRADITION OF ANTI–INTELLECTUALISM DENIES that man's chief attribute is reason. At the very height of her career, when the goddess Reason was enthroned in the Cathedral of Notre Dame, she suffered her severest metaphysical assault at the hands of Immanuel Kant on the other side of the Rhine. In Kant's view, human reason was too feeble to pierce the mystery at the core of reality, too myopic to lead us to truths beyond the world of sense experience: "It is not equipped with wings strong enough to part the lofty clouds which hide from our eyes the secrets of the other world." Reason can gives us technical knowledge but cannot make us better or wiser. Kant disputed her transcendental claims as a source of morality or final court of appeal in the ultimate questions of reality and confined her authority to the limits of the empirical world. There is no escape from the haunted chamber of the mind in which we are imprisoned, and it is futile to beat against its bolted doors. Of all the images of incarceration to describe man's earthly existence—Plato's cave, the body as the soul's sepulchre, the ivory tower, the whale's belly—the severest is that derived from Kant's philosophy.

After much introspection, reason disqualified herself as *non compos mentis,* unable to carry on the business of the mind, and handed over her functions and prerogatives to language, the repository of the intuitive wisdom of the race. But it was soon discovered that language itself was corrupt, "zerfressen bis auf die Knochen" (Fritz Mauthner), and unfit for the appropriation of knowledge or as a guide for human experience.

This persistent theme of the poet, that his work is more significant and enduring than that of the man of action (the theme of *exegi monumentum* in Horace, Pushkin and Shakespeare: *Sonnets,* 56, 65), leads to exaggerated pride and confidence in his intellectual gifts which he tends to value above moral virtues. The poet is envied even by kings, for he gives their deeds imperishable form in stone and sound and makes them immortal (the subject of Browning's poem *Cleon*). Balzac wrote under the picture of his contemporary, Napoleon, the proud words: "What he could not achieve with the sword, I shall accomplish with the pen."

There is the famous case of Georg Kaiser, the leading dramatist of German expressionism in the days after the First World War, who, in a sensational trial, defended his theft of rugs from a villa he had rented on the grounds that he was a distinguished artist and not to be judged by the same rules as others. He was nevertheless sentenced to several months in jail. This prolific writer of social dramas was married to Margarethe Habenicht, who, despite her name, had brought him a substantial dowry which enabled him to live in luxury for a number of years. At the trial he claimed exemption from paying his debts in the name of his artistic genius, ending his defense with the following statement:

> I hold myself to be an extravagantly exceptional case. The law does not apply to me. The obligation I have to myself is higher than my obligation to the law. . . . The idea that everybody is equal before the law is

nonsensical. I am not everybody. I am great, therefore I am permitted to break the law. Even though I might be considered childish, I must declare that I am unspeakably great! My arrest is not only a personal disaster. It is a national disaster. The flags should have been flown at half-mast.

The artist is thus not bound by the conventional morality that binds the less gifted part of mankind, a view that is likewise defended by one of the characters in Dostoyevski's *The Devils* as follows:

> Shakespeare and Raphael are higher than the emancipation of the serfs, higher than nationalism, higher than socialism, higher than the younger generation, higher than chemistry, higher even than almost all humanity, for they are the fruit of all mankind, and perhaps the highest fruition that can possibly exist.

Those who elevate geniuses and their works above the moral law argue, for example, that Goethe's love poems compensate us for the wrecked feminine lives that inspired them. Carlyle stated that he was prepared to sacrifice the lives of a million Englishmen (excluding his own) for one Shakespeare. The German historian Treitschke was of the opinion that the statues of Phidias, the greatest artist of the Periclean Age, were ample compensation for the slavery that supported the culture of ancient Greece. This famous scholar might have modified his views had he himself been sent into slavery for several years and then be compelled to gaze all day at ancient statues in a Berlin museum. If a fire were to break out in a museum, would Treitschke save a famous painting, e.g., the Mona Lisa, in preference to the lives of entrapped visitors, even if these included members of his own family? This *ad hominem* argument may not affect the soundness of his view, although his moral stand would be more convincing had he been prepared to make a personal sacrifice to support it. Is one justified in deliberately sacrificing others to achieve a revolutionary ideal of social utopia? Has human life infinite value, higher than all cultural values? Are there not values higher than life itself that are worth preserving? (We feel that we are not justified in sacrificing individual persons we happen to know, but we constantly make decisions which we know will cause the death of many, perhaps millions, of our fellowmen.)

At the end of their lives, however, poets and philosophers often despair of their joyless existence, feeling that they have been duped by the bold harlot (language) who had promised them the fruit of the Tree of Knowledge and given them empty words instead. After an unequal struggle with reality they realize that they did nothing to alter human nature or alleviate human suffering, and they turn from complacency to dejection, from indolence to despair, often accompanied by thoughts of self-destruction:

> We poets in our youth begin in gladness;
> But thereof come in the end despondency and madness.
> —Wordsworth, *Resolution and Independence,* VII

About the middle of the last century the exaggerated self-worship of the writer turned into a feeling of self-pity at having bartered away his heavenly gifts for the acclaim of a materialistic society. Many writers and poets in the past had ended their lives on the same regretful note, the futility of a life devoted to writing, recalling Plato's observation in *Phaedrus:* "The only valuable way to write is to inscribe justice and beauty on a soul." At the end of his days Virgil looked back on a long life in the service of "that cursed and affected fraud called Art," renounced his ambition to fame and greatness and retired to live the life of a simple farmer. Philosophers are not exempt from this feeling of futility. Thomas Aquinas in his last years abandoned his studies, confessing that they seemed to him like so much straw, and sought to comprehend the truth of life by mere living. Adam Smith before his death directed that all his manuscripts, except for a few selected essays, be committed to the flames. Sir Humphry Davy, one of England's greatest scientists, confessed on his deathbed that all his inventions meant little to him, including his safety lamp that had saved the lives of many miners. David Hume, whose ruling passion was the love of literary fame, despaired of the prospect of ever attaining truth and certainty by means of philosophy with its interminable disputes, errors and absurdities and decided to live like all other men according to the world's general maxims:

> I dine, I play a game of backgammon, I converse, and am merry with my friends; and when, after three or four hours' amusement, I would return to these speculations, they appear so cold, so strained, and ridiculous, that I cannot find in my heart to enter into them any further. . . . I am ready to throw all my books and papers into the fire, and resolve never more to renounce the pleasures of life for the sake of reasoning and philosophy.

By the end of the century there arose in Germany a tradition of inexpressibility *(Unaussprechlichkeitstradition)*. The characters in novels and dramas lived in an atmosphere in which they could hardly breathe, an atmosphere full of mis-hearings, repetitions, incoherent phrases and long pauses, typographically indicated by dots, dashes and asterisks, as if speaking to each other through a *fenestra locutaria,* the window through which heremetic nuns talk to the outside world. Many writers avoided the transcription of dialogue altogether and turned to interior monologue or lyrical drama in which the characters speak their pieces and make their exits.

Language is not only a poor conveyer of the truth, as we see in Browning's *The Ring and the Book* (1869) with its interminable discussion of a murder as perceived from different points of view. It is also inadequate to express strong emotions, as already described in Shelley's drama *The Cenci* (1819) where the matter of a rape is hushed up in the very first line: "If I try to speak I shall go mad." A cloak of silence is thrown over the unspeakable deed in an attempt to exclude it from reality, and its horror intimated by nonverbal communication, gestures, penetrating looks.

The disillusion of writers in the power of language to express reality received its most powerful form in Hugo von Hofmannsthal's *Letter to Lord Chandos,* written in the early part of the century. In this "Letter" the author, one of the most gifted writers of his day, describes the deep gloom that descended upon him when he suddenly discovered that his language could no longer be relied upon to apprehend the world in which he lived. Vertigo invaded his senses when he looked at the page before him. The sentences had lost their agglutinative power; the rebellious parts of speech ran wild on the page, nouns seeking their lost qualifiers, pronouns their antecedents, and verbs their paradigms. The whole edifice of his life's work that had rested on faith in the ultimate correspondence of word and thing had now crumbled before his very eyes. Unable to use his native tongue to express his thoughts, he looked at the page with mute contempt and began to search for some strange tongue whose words were unknown to him, "a tongue in which dumb things speak to me . . . and in which I shall be able to justify myself before an unknown Judge."

The search for "a tongue in which dumb things speak" developed into a literary cult of dumbness. Many writers and artists left their middle-class homes of respectable conformity to live among primitive people in an atmosphere, it was thought, of silent simplicity. Lafcadio Hearn fled to Japan, Gauguin to Tahiti, D.H. Lawrence to the Indians of New Mexico; George Borrow wrote admiringly about wandering gypsies, and Bret Harte about the outcasts in the mining towns of California. But they found neither the peace nor solitude they had sought, for they took with them their past lives, their habits, hopes and memories. Despite tourist brochures, primitive societies no longer provide a refuge for civilized man, having been gradually contaminated by the byproducts of technical progress. Even the desert, once the refuge of anchorites and prophets, has now become the testing ground for the ultimate weapons of destruction (Ger. *Wüste,* desert, has become the ground, literally and etymologically, of *Verwüstung* devastation). The literary cult of dumbness then found inspiration in the pathological mutterings of the feeble minded. The first literary work that had an inarticulate primitive as the principal character was Georg Büchner's drama *Woyzeck* (1836). Only a few years before the production of this play there was the sensational case of Kaspar Hauser, the speechless wolf-boy who was suddenly seen in the streets of Nuremberg, exciting great interest among philosophers and linguists who studied his elementary grunts in search of clues to the origin of human speech. These studies, however, yielded little scientific information concerning man's original state and development, although it inspired a number of imaginary literary creations, including a poem by Paul Verlaine, a novel by Jakob Wassermann and an ingenious play by Peter Handtke. And finally, as we have seen, the writer turned to the dumb beasts of the field in search of peace and speechless felicity.

Dissatisfaction with language as the ideal mediator between the world of sense and the spirit was the dominant theme of the entire century. Verbal discourse was suspect. The silent images of the spirit elude articulation in words; words obscure direct vision and impede the soul's ascent. The realm of words is not the realm of meaning. Goethe, one of the supreme masters of language, wrote at the height of his literary career:

> We talk far too much. We should talk less and draw more. I personally should like to renounce speech altogether and, like organic Nature, communicate everything I have to say in sketches. That fig tree, this little snake, the cocoon on my window sill quietly awaiting its future—all these are momentous signatures. A person able to decipher their meaning properly would soon be able to dispense with the written or the spoken word altogether. The more I think of it, there is something futile, mediocre, even (I am tempted to say) foppish about speech. By contrast, how the gravity of Nature and her silence startle you, when you stand face to face with her, undistracted, before a barren ridge or in the desolation of the ancient hills.
> (Quoted from Aldous Huxley, *The Doors of Perception*, New York, 1954, pp. 73f.)

Goethe's pictorial naturalism pointed the way to a romantic theory that transformed the world into a formless stream perceived by pure intuition unmediated by language, progressively relapsing into an irrationalism that became the dominant mood of German intellectual life.

With the renunciation of human speech as a vehicle of communication, the word forfeited its function as the bearer of meaning and proclaimed its essence in the elemental power of the sound alone. In the last chapter of Hawthorne's *The Scarlet Letter*, Hester Prynne, while listening to a sermon in the courtyard of the overfilled church, is overcome by the preacher's resonant voice which reached her ears unencumbered by "the grosser medium of words." In things that mattered most the spoken word became more and more impotent: "Let him who has something to say step forward, and keep silent" (Karl Kraus). Dostoyevski's Grand Inquisitor is met by the majestic silence of a mute Christ. In the century that followed, a century filled with unspeakable terror and violence, a stony silence descended on the poet, the mouthpiece of the world. In his brief poem, *33 konstellationen,* the disillusioned German poet, Eugen Grominger, advises his fellow-poets to remain silent:

> schweigen schweigen schweigen
> schweigen schweigen schweigen
> schweigen   schweigen
> schweigen schweigen schweigen
> schweigen schweigen schweigen

—a piece of advice followed by Louis Aragon, who summed up the desolate mood of his generation in his poem aptly called *Suicide:*

> A b c d e f
>   g h i j k l
>   m n o p q r
>   s t u v w
>   x y z

On the other hand, those who acknowledge the primacy of human reason retain confidence in language to define and illumine our lives. To despair of the intelligible forms of human speech because they are found to be inadequate to grasp reality is to remove the very basis of thought itself, as if fish should complain of the water that supports them or, to use a Kantian image, a dove should decide to fly without the air that seems to impede its flight. The voice of reason may be faint, but it is insistent and will in the end bear away the victory. Better Socrates in prison than Caliban on the throne! To permit instinct and sentiment to extend their influence over man's rational mind is to debase his speculative powers and set him adrift on a dark ocean of matter without rule or compass:

> And, hark, what discord follows! . . . .
> Then every thing includes itself in power,
> Power into will, will into appetite;
> And appetite, an universal wolf,
> So doubly seconded with will and power,
> Must make perforce an universal prey,
> And last eat up himself.
> —Ulysses in *Troilus and Cressida*

The disastrous consequences of man's renunciation of reason is depicted in one of Goya's *Caprichos* that bears the caption: "The dream of reason produces monsters" (1799). This etching (see next page) is the counterpart to the Naming Scene in the first chapter where Adam appears as a scholar armed with quill and scroll on his way to freedom and self-discovery. His fundamental allegiance from the very outset is to the life of the intellect and the world of ideas. He comes forward with a claim upon our *minds,* with a desire to communicate and win our assent. In the beginning was the Word, the Mind, rational Thought. In Goya's etching, on the other hand, we see man at the end of his tether, a pathetic figure sprawled across the desk in a fitful sleep, surrounded by malevolent cats, bats and owls. Man, the heir to glory and but little lower than the angels, here appears as no more than "a sack of dung" (St. Bernard), "the garbage can of the universe" (Pascal), trapped in a terrifying world from which God has withdrawn, a world of madmen, executioners, dungeons and concentration camps.

Man's first task on awakening from this nightmare of history will be to ask himself Hamlet's question: to be or not to be, whether he wants to go on living as an individual and as a species. Will he be able to rebuild his wrecked house on a metaphysically condemned site? What could he still salvage to regain his lost unity and sense of

El sueño de la razon
produce monstruos.

Caprichos *43*. [536]
1797-98

direction? Did he succumb to irrational ideologies, or did he perish from wounds inflicted by his overbearing reason? Was his faith too feeble to make room for the life of the mind, or was his rational mind too proud to bow to knowledge perceived by faith? These are the questions that have perplexed man ever since he came blinking out of Plato's cave in ancient Greece, questions that will continue to perplex him as long as he is bound to the hard crust of the earth where perishable matter is wedded to spirit and where body and soul are locked in perpetual battle.

There is no road back to the virginal life of Eden whose gates are now guarded by cherubim with flaming swords. Yet a faint reflection of the radiance of his lost home remained in man. He did not expire at the Garden gate. He found enough strength to plant the cypress in the stony waste and raise the standard of humanity amid chaos. Like Jacob, with his head on a stone pillow, he could still dream of heaven. All was not lost! The dark seed still grows into the stately oak. Leaves wither and fall but are eternally renewed. Tyranny reigns but the moral law shines (dimly) through the mists of passion and ignorance. Here at the steep juncture between the glory and the dark, between the crepuscle of a world that is lost and one yet unborn, where Eden is but a memory and a hope, man can still view the mighty drama of life with fortitude and learn

> to bear all naked truths
> And to envisage all circumstance, all calm,
> This is the top of sovereignty.
> —John Keats

This is the testimony God left in Adam's flawed but proud seed, a testimony that shall remain until man completes his probation on earth and awakens to another level of existence on the thither side of corruption where the soul is untouched by the terrors of the flesh, where merit, virtue and reward are weighed in scales other than those of this pitiless world. The loathsome mask will fall from man's face as he becomes "Scepterless, free, uncircumscribed . . . equal, unclassed, tribeless and nationless,/ Exempt from awe, worship, degree, the king/ Over himself; just, gentle, wise" (Shelley). The eyes of the body will then be one with the eyes of the mind (Hegel), and the labors of Martha one with the meditations of Mary; the cut worm will forgive the plow, and the lamb the butcher's knife (Blake). The black cross of mortification will then blend with the white roses of faith that surround it

(Luther's seal), faithfulness will spring up from the ground and righteousness look down from the sky (Ps. 85:11), and men shall see all things as God who, leaning over the parapet of his celestial gazebo, sees the whole world in a single glance, at once swift, minute and panoramic.